Wildfire Island Docs

Welcome to Paradise!

Meet the small but dedicated team of medics who service the remote Pacific Wildfire Island.

In this idyllic setting relationships are rekindled, passions are stirred, and bonds that will last a lifetime are forged in the tropical heat…

But there's also a darker side to paradise—secrets, lies and greed amidst the Lockhart family threaten the community, and the team find themselves fighting to save more than the lives of their patients. They must band together to fight for the future of the island they've all come to call home!

Read Caroline and Keanu's story in
The Man She Could Never Forget
by Meredith Webber

Read Anna and Luke's story in
The Nurse Who Stole His Heart
by Alison Roberts

Read Maddie and Josh's story in
Saving Maddie's Baby
by Marion Lennox

Read Sarah and Harry's story in
A Sheikh to Capture Her Heart
by Meredith Webber

Read Lia and Sam's story in
The Fling That Changed Everything
by Alison Roberts

Read Hettie and Max's story in
A Child to Open Their Hearts
by Marion Lennox

All available now!

Dear Reader,

Confession time…I love a bit of drama!

And what better place for it than our fabulous M'Langi islands?

I couldn't wait to get back there again, and this time I got to unleash a tropical storm that's a perfect backdrop to the powerful attraction that neither Lia nor Sam are looking for but find themselves unable to ignore.

Is it a simple story of two people unexpectedly finding their soulmates in a tropical paradise?

Of course not.

There's a reason Lia's come to Wildfire Island, and it has nothing to do with Sam. And Sam…? Well, he's got some baggage, and he doesn't realise how much it's still affecting him.

It's a bit of a wild ride. I loved writing it and I hope you enjoy it just as much.

With love,

Alison xxx

THE FLING THAT CHANGED EVERYTHING

BY

ALISON ROBERTS

Published in Great Britain 2016
By Mills & Boon, an imprint of HarperCollins*Publishers*
1 London Bridge Street, London, SE1 9GF

ISBN: 978-0-263-26406-7

Our policy is to use papers that are natural, renewable and recyclable products and made from wood grown in sustainable forests. The logging [illegible] conform to the legal environmental [illegible] origin

Printed and bound in Great Britain
by CPI Antony Rowe, Chippenham, Wiltshire

Alison Roberts is a New Zealander, currently lucky enough to live near a beautiful beach in Auckland. She is also lucky enough to write for both the Mills & Boon Romance and Medical Romance lines. A primary school teacher in a former life, she is also a qualified paramedic. She loves to travel and dance, drink champagne and spend time with her daughter and her friends.

Books by Alison Roberts

Mills & Boon Medical Romance

The Honourable Maverick
Sydney Harbour Hospital: Zoe's Baby
Falling for Her Impossible Boss
The Legendary Playboy Surgeon
St Piran's: The Wedding
Maybe This Christmas...?
NYC Angels: An Explosive Reunion
Always the Hero
From Venice with Love
200 Harley Street: The Proud Italian
A Little Christmas Magic
Always the Midwife
Daredevil, Doctor...Husband?
The Nurse Who Stole His Heart

Visit the Author Profile page at millsandboon.co.uk for more titles.

Praise for
Alison Roberts

'...the author gave me wonderful enjoyable moments of conflict and truth-revealing moments of joy and sorrow...I highly recommend this book for all lovers of romance with medical drama as a backdrop and second-chance love.'

—*Contemporary Romance Reviews* on
NYC Angels: An Explosive Reunion

'This is a deeply emotional book, dealing with difficult life and death issues and situations in the medical community. But it is also a powerful story of love, forgiveness and learning to be intimate... There's a lot packed into this novella. I'm impressed.'

—*Goodreads* on
200 Harley Street: The Proud Italian

CHAPTER ONE

THE SOUND OF the telephone ringing could barely be heard over the cacophony as the Roselli family gathered in their kitchen for dinner.

It wasn't a big room. If the whole family had been here, they would have had to use the huge, rustic table out in the courtyard, beneath the vine-smothered pergola, but it was raining today—the kind of tropical downpour that was familiar to people living in Northern Australia—and the vines weren't enough protection from the wet.

So, here they were, piling into the kitchen that was a long room, where Adriana Roselli presided over the benchtop and oven at one end and the scrubbed pine table that could fit ten people—if they squeezed up—filled the other end of the room. Fitting a wheelchair in made it a little more complicated, of course, and that was why the noise level was so high right now.

'*Ow*... You ran over my foot, Fiona. Watch where you're going.'

'If you didn't have your stupid ears full of your horrible music, you would have seen us coming. Move *yourself*, Guy.'

'Not until you say you're sorry. You've probably broken my toe.'

'You're the one who should apologise. Look, you've made Angel *cry…*'

'Look out, all of you. If I drop this lasagne, you'll all be sorry. *Mamma mia…*' Adriana held a vast steaming tray over her head as her youngest son elbowed his way past her. 'Why don't my children ever grow up and act their ages? What have I ever done to deserve this? Lia, why isn't the bread on the table?'

'I'm coming… Oh, is that the *phone*?'

It took a moment for the effect of her words to sink in. Adriana almost dropped the lasagne onto the centre of her table and then covered her mouth with her hands, her gaze—like that of everyone else in the room, apart from Angel—swivelling towards Nico.

Was this the call they'd all been waiting for today?

'I'll get it.'

'No, I will.'

'It'll be for Nico. Let *him* get it.'

But Nico was looking like a possum caught in headlights—too scared to move.

'I'll get it.' Lia shoved the long basket piled with fragrant homemade bread at her brother Guy, but he had his eyes shut, his head nodding to whatever mesmerising beat he was still listening to, and she was too late, anyway. Her younger sister, Elena, had reached the phone first.

'Lia? It's for you.'

'What?' Lia shook her head. Who would be calling her on her day off? Her life consisted of her work and her family and that was it. One glance around the room would have been more than enough to remind her of why there was no room for anything else. And she wouldn't want it any other way, either. This was her home and her heart all wrapped up in one delicious-smelling, messy, noisy parcel. She loved every person here so much it could be a physical ache.

'Tell them to call back, then. I'm busy.'

She put the bread on the table beside one of the salads, smiling at her father, who was already in his place at the head of the table, silently waiting for chaos to morph into a more civilised mealtime. She glanced at the place settings Elena had been put in charge of. Where was the special, modified cutlery that Angel needed if she was going to feed herself?

'It's Bruce,' Elena shouted. 'And he says it's important.'

Bruce? Her boss at the ambulance station? More than her boss, in fact. He'd been the one to push her into her specialised training that had given her the qualifications to gain her dream job on the helicopter crew. He was her mentor and a good friend. If Bruce said something was important, it was.

Were they calling in extra crew for some major disaster?

'Coming…' The noise level around her was rising again but Lia was barely aware of the small spat as her mother pulled the ear buds away from Guy. Or that Fiona was berating Elena for forgetting the special cutlery. She couldn't miss that Nico was staring into space and clearly needed some reassurance or that her father's silence was deeper than his customary patience, but paying attention to those things would have to wait.

'Bruce?' Lia pushed her long, unruly curls out of

the way and pressed the phone to her ear so that she could hear properly. 'Hi. What's up?'

The noise level was still too high to hear properly so Lia slipped out of the kitchen and into the hallway.

'Say that again. You want me to do *what…*?'

The silence was one of the things Sam Taylor loved best about Wildfire Island. Especially at this time of day, when the sun was almost gone and the scent of tropical flowers grew so much stronger.

He drew in a deep breath, shutting his eyes for a moment. And then he opened them and looked out from the vantage point he had chosen to the ocean surrounding this island, which had been his home ever since he'd begun working at the hospital here several years ago.

He'd taken the highest road on the island as he'd walked from the hospital and now he was on ground that was above the gold mine that had been the catalyst for so many people besides the islanders being able to call this place home. To one side he caught a glimpse of the village and the rocky promontory with the little church on top. He couldn't see over the cliff tops to Sunset Beach on the other side, but this wasn't an evening to chill out, watching the fiery show on the cliffs that had given the island its European name, anyway. Dense clouds were scudding sideways, intermittently hiding the sun, and it wouldn't be long before they joined forces and unleashed the kind of tropical downpour that was a regular feature of the cyclone season.

Maybe it was that atmospheric tension that had pushed him into taking this strenuous walk after a busy day that had left him feeling physically jaded. They were short-staffed at the moment and having Jack, the helicopter pilot, take one of his nurses on a mission had made things a lot more stressful. It was a good thing that the plane was due in tomorrow, bringing in some new FIFO—fly in, fly out—personnel. And this time there would be a paramedic as well as a nurse so he would not only have extra hands in the hospital, they wouldn't get borrowed just when they were needed in Theatre or something.

He let his breath out in a long sigh and felt more of the tension ebb. He could always find peace in this view. Excitement, even, as he looked out at the darkening shapes that were the outlying islands. The biggest one, Atangi, had been settled for the longest time and had the infrastructure of shops and schools. He could see the misty outline of islands that he knew well due to the clinics they ran on places like French Island. He could see the tiny humps of the uninhabited ones, too, and one of them was now his own.

How lucky was it that so many tradesmen had come to the islands to work on the upgrade of the laboratory and conference facilities that was now a feature of Wildfire Island? He'd been able to quietly offer some of them more work, building his dream house and the jetty for his yacht on a bush-covered island paradise that he had yet to name.

In the not-too-distant future, he wouldn't be walking home to the accommodation provided for both the permanent and FIFO staff that kept the hospital and clinics running in this remote area. He'd take a boat and go home to picture-perfect solitude and the sheer beauty of nature. Not his yacht, of course. As much as he loved sailing, he'd have to be able to travel fast to get back here in an emergency, so he was looking at getting a new speedboat. An inflatable, probably.

For some reason, though, the prospect of that beauty and solitude wasn't generating the excitement it usually did.

For the first time, it was actually casting a shadow of doubt on if he was doing the right thing.

Was it the remnants of a hectic day that made him think it wouldn't be a good idea to have even a small strip of ocean between himself and the hospital? What if he hadn't been there to deal with that anaphylaxis from a bee sting that had seen a young mother terrified that she was about to lose her child? Or if they hadn't been able to perform that emergency appendectomy before the infected organ burst and could have caused a life-threatening sepsis?

Or was it the storm brewing? The wind picking up and those bad-tempered-looking clouds just waiting for an excuse to spark an outburst?

No. It felt deeper than anything as external as work or the weather. The shadow was more like an empty space in his soul. The alone space.

But he'd come here to this remote part of the Pacific Ocean to escape in the first place, and being alone was the ultimate escape, wasn't it?

Turning away from the view, Sam automatically looked around, forgetting for a moment that he hadn't brought Bugsy with him this time. The dog was a part of the hospital family here, and his care was shared amongst others, including him, when his owner was back on the mainland. One of the nurses had him today so Sam hadn't had the pleasure of taking him out for his daily walk.

That's what it was, he decided. That's why he had this sudden, inexplicable sense of loneliness.

Maybe it was time he got a canine companion of his own. A Portuguese water dog, perhaps, who would love boats and fishing expeditions and swimming at the tiny, perfect beach that had been why he'd fallen in love with the island he now owned.

That way he'd have the best job in the world in a place where he could live happily ever after, and he'd have company to share it with. Company that would expect no more of him than his love.

What more could anybody want?

There was only one chair empty at the table as Lia went back into the kitchen. Plates were being passed, laden with the delicious layers of meat and cheese and pasta that had given Adriana Roselli's lasagne its well-deserved reputation of being the best.

'What did Bruce want?' Elena reached for a thick, warm slice of bread and added it to her plate. 'Was he asking you out for a date?'

'Bruce is old enough to be my father,' Lia said sternly. 'And I'm old enough to know how ridiculous that would be.'

'Oh, give it a rest,' Elena snapped. 'Mike's only thirty-nine.'

'And you're only twenty-six. Thirteen years, Lena. Count them. It's almost a generation.'

'At least I've *got* a boyfriend. You're turning into an old maid, Lia.'

'That's enough,' Adriana ordered. 'Sit down, Lia. Eat. You're far too skinny these days. I can see your bones from here.'

Lia ignored the comments from both her mother and her sister. She slid into the seat beside Angel's wheelchair.

'Look at the way you're holding your spoon, darling. Good girl… Don't forget to blow on it. That lasagne looks hot.' She leaned sideways to demonstrate but Angel giggled and tipped her spoon and the food fell off to land on her lap.

'Thanks for that, Lia.' But Angel's mother, her sister Fiona, was smiling as she wiped up the small accident. 'Let's try that again, shall we, Angel?'

'So what *did* Bruce want?' Nico was picking at his food and clearly hoping for a distraction from his own thoughts.

'He offered me a job for two weeks. On a helicopter crew on an island about two hundred miles northwest of Cairns. It's called Wildfire.'

'An island?' Adriana shook her head. '*Pff*…what for? A holiday?'

'There's a hospital there, Mamma. It looks after a big population of people over a huge area. Bruce said it would be great experience for me. I'd have to do things I'd probably never get the chance to do here. And, if I liked it, I could go onto a regular roster to fly in for two-week stints.'

'You can't go,' Elena declared. 'Nico's going to be going into hospital for his surgery any day now and you know what Mamma's like around hospitals. You're the only one who can explain things properly and stop her crying. And even if you're here for the operation, what about the chemo? It'll be horrendous.'

'No, it won't.' Lia sent her sister a warning glance before turning to smile at her brother. 'You're going to fly through this, Nico. I know it's scary but testicular cancer has a really high cure rate and you're going to be one of those success stories. It'll be okay.'

'Promise?' Nico, like the rest of the family, looked to Lia as his medical expert.

Lia's smile was one of genuine reassurance. 'Promise.' Even if the treatment didn't go as well as hoped, she would make it okay. Somehow.

'Do you want to go?' Fiona's query was sceptical.

'It would be exciting,' Lia admitted. 'Even the name of the island is cool. Wildfire...'

'They have fires?' Adriana shook her head. 'You don't want to go somewhere that has fires.'

'Wildfire Island? Wasn't that in the news not long ago?' Guy put down his fork to fish his phone out of his pocket. 'I'm sure I heard something about a mine exploding or something.'

'Well, that's that.' The spoon clanked against the crockery dish as if Adriana's statement was final. 'I'm not having you going off into exploding mines.'

'No, it didn't explode.' Guy sounded disappointed. 'Just collapsed. People got hurt and there was a big rescue mission but it's okay now. And why would Lia be going down a mine, anyway?'

'I wouldn't,' Lia said reassuringly. 'And what makes it really attractive is what they pay. I'd earn three times what I usually do in a fortnight. Imagine how far that would get us in buying those new walking aids for Angel.'

'No...' Adriana handed a laden plate to Lia. 'It still sounds dangerous. Flying helicopters around islands miles from anywhere? What if you crash?'

'It's no different from what I do here. Apparently

the head pilot is someone Bruce knows and he's top of his game. It's my job, Mamma—you know that. And I love it.'

'It's not natural,' Adriana sighed. 'You're thirty-two, Lia. You should be married and having *bambinos* by now. Look at your sister. She was a *mamma* already by your age.'

'Mmm.' Lia and Fiona shared a rueful glance that took in how well that had worked out. Angel had been born prematurely and the lack of oxygen during a difficult birth had been responsible for her cerebral palsy. Her father had walked out of their lives as soon as he'd learned of her disability.

'The money's amazing.' Guy spoke with his mouth full. 'I'd do it if I were you. Hey...you could get the roof fixed and I wouldn't have to trip over that bucket in my bedroom every time it rains.'

Her father had been silent throughout the discussion, his gaze on his plate, but he looked up as Guy spoke and Lia could see the shame in his eyes.

It's not your fault, she told him silently, her heart breaking. *And you'll get another job before the redundancy money runs out.*

The words she spoke aloud were very different. A daughter asking her father's advice.

'What do you reckon, Dad? Should I go?'

He returned her smile and the warmth in his eyes told her that her reassurance had been received and appreciated.

'If you want to do it, *cara*, you should.'

Lia nodded slowly. 'I think I do.'

'Mamma mia.' Adriana crossed herself as she closed her eyes. 'When would you leave?'

'Um…tomorrow. It seems like the person who was going to go has had an accident at the last minute, which is why Bruce was asked to find someone else. He's happy to give me leave.'

The reality of the offer was sinking in around the table and everyone was staring at Lia with a mix of admiration and trepidation.

'I said I'd call him back as soon as I'd discussed it with the family. Nico? You get to have the final vote. If you want me to be here for your surgery, I'll say no.'

'Go,' Nico said. 'I'll have more than enough family fussing over me. I'm only going to be in hospital for a couple of days. You can send me some cool pictures and I can boast about my fabulous sister who's off doing brave stuff and saving the world.'

Lia grinned. 'You're on. Right…' She scooped in a hurried mouthful of her dinner. 'I'd better go and ring Bruce back and start packing. I'll have to be at the airport at five-thirty in the morning.'

'I'll drive you.'

Her father smiled as he spoke but her mother burst into tears. For a moment Lia considered changing her mind but then she glanced at Angel and remembered what that extra money could mean.

Swallowing hard, she pushed back her chair and went to make the phone call.

'Whoa…' Jack Richards, Wildfire Island's head helicopter pilot, pushed his sunglasses down his nose to peer over the top of them. 'You seeing what I'm seeing, Sam?'

Two young people had climbed out of the small plane and were heading across the tarmac to where they were waiting in the shade. The man had to be the paramedic, Sam decided, so no wonder Jack had elbowed him in the ribs. The new FIFO nurse was a stunner, all right. Tall and lean, she had a mane of curly dark hair that the wind was playing havoc with and legs that seemed to go on forever beneath the short shorts she was wearing. Huge sunglasses were hiding half her face but even from this distance you could see a generous mouth that was clearly designed for laughing.

Or kissing, perhaps…?

Maybe it was just as well she'd be safely confined to the hospital during working hours and not floating around remote islands with a good-looking young helicopter pilot. Romantic liaisons with FIFO staff happened—of course they did—and Jack was not shy about enjoying the opportunities, but for Sam it was a no-no. He'd always kept any such casual hook-ups to the times when he was on a break a long way away from here. This was his home and, as such, it was too important to mess with by indulging in something that he'd seen lead to long-lasting negative fallouts in others.

He didn't need the clipboard he was holding to remind him that this was work time. Supplies were being unloaded from the small plane that was their regular link with the mainland of Australia and, amongst them would be the important medical packs containing drugs and all the other items Sam had ordered. They'd run low on dressings and suture packs after an unusually high number of minor trauma incidents in the past couple of weeks.

'Let's check that everything we ordered has come

in,' he said to Jack. 'We don't want to hold up the pilot in this weather.'

The wind had picked up even as they walked towards the plane.

'G'day, mate.' Sam extended a hand towards the male newcomer. 'I'm Sam Taylor—one of the permanent doctors at the hospital here.'

'Good to meet you. I'm Matt.'

'Welcome to Wildfire Island. Is this your first FIFO experience?'

'Sure is.' Matt's smile was rueful. 'Might be the last, too, after that flight.'

'Oh, come on, Matt.' The girl was now restraining her hair with both hands to keep it from covering her face. 'It was fun.'

Her grin suggested that a bumpy ride had been a bonus and Sam couldn't help grinning back. A young woman who was gutsy as well as gorgeous? What man wouldn't appreciate that combination of attributes?

'I'm Lia Roselli.' She had to let go of her hair with one hand as she extended it to shake Sam's. The wind snatched the tumble of dark curls and plastered it across her face and she was laughing as she scraped it free.

The sound was as attractive as the rest of her. No wonder Jack was grinning like an idiot. It was only then that he realised that his own mouth was still widely stretched. It was an effort, in fact, to pull his lips back into line.

'I've got a hair tie somewhere.' Lia delved into the soft leather shoulder bag she was carrying. 'Sorry, I should have tried to arrive looking a bit more professional, shouldn't have I?'

'You weren't to know there's a cyclone brewing.'

Jack turned to her after shaking Matt's hand. 'I'm Jack Richards.'

'Oh…you're my pilot.' The search for the hair tie was abandoned as Lia took his hand. 'Awesome. I'm looking forward to working with you.'

'You're the *paramedic*?'

Sam didn't mean to sound so astonished. He deserved the look he got from both the newcomers. Even Jack's eyebrows shot up. In just a few words he'd managed to make it sound like he not only had a prejudice against male nurses but that he didn't think females were up to the kind of dangerous work that helicopter paramedicine could throw at them. He didn't think either of those things. If he was really honest, the tone had probably come from disappointment more than surprise, and what was that about? Even the nurses tucked safely away in the hospital were not immune to Jack's charm, so what chance did Lia have?

Good grief… Was that oddly unsettling flash something other than disappointment? Jealousy, even?

'Sam didn't get the memo.' Jack was trying to rescue him. 'And, I have to admit, it's the first time we've had a female paramedic as a FIFO.'

'First time for a male nurse, too?' Matt was smiling. 'Good thing we've come, then, isn't it, Lia? Time the glass ceilings were broken around here.'

They all laughed, which broke the awkwardness. The distraction of having to check the delivered supplies off against the order form took a few more minutes and by the time the FIFOs' luggage was brought out from the back of the compartment, Sam was ready to make amends for his faux pas.

'It is a good thing,' he told Matt as the new nurse retrieved his backpack. 'We're trying to encourage more islanders to train as nurses and you'll be a role model that might open a few eyes. How would you feel about dropping into the high school over on Atangi and giving a bit of a career talk?'

'I'm up for anything,' Matt said. 'I love my job and I'd be only too happy to encourage the lads.'

'Hey…I love my job, too.' Lia was beaming at Sam. 'Maybe I could come and inspire the girls?'

Jack was grinning again. 'You up for anything, too, huh?'

The flirting was unmistakeable. The flick of the long braid Lia now had her hair confined to was also an obvious message. And she could deal with more than the weather.

'Anything professional.' Her tone was a warning. Romance had been the last thing on her mind when she'd decided to take this job. It was the last thing on her mind any time these days, thanks to the time and emotional energy her family required. And even if she had been interested in meeting someone, it wouldn't be Jack. She'd met his type too many times before. Dated them. Been dumped and hurt when they moved on—as they always did if it looked like the girl was getting serious.

Had she been too abrupt? Lia softened her tone. 'I'm up for the new experience and if I like it I'll come back next time. Sounds like the guy I'm replacing got a nasty leg fracture and won't be back for a while.'

'I told him paragliding was a dodgy hobby.' Jack reached out as if he was going to offer to carry Lia's pack but then changed his mind and adjusted his sunglasses instead.

Sam hid a smile. So Lia *could* look after herself.

'Not that he wasn't good at it.' Jack seemed to be scanning the clouds now. 'Just got unlucky, I guess.'

'Lucky for me…' Lia hoisted her backpack as if it weighed nothing. 'Especially the timing. Who knew they paid so much more for coming here in the cyclone season?'

Sam's inner smile vanished without a trace. The disconcerted look on Lia's face made him realise that something of what he was feeling must be showing but he didn't care. He had better reason than most *not* to care about someone to whom money was all-important, hadn't he? He turned away.

'Let's go,' he told Matt. 'I'll show you your accommodation and then give you a tour of the hospital.'

What had just happened there?

Lia had her backpack settled onto her shoulders and she was ready to go. Didn't she have accommodation to see? Wouldn't a tour of at least the emergency department of the hospital be appropriate for someone who could be delivering seriously unwell people to a place that might be short on staff experienced in dealing with resuscitation?

Maybe it had something to do with that very unsubtle attempt at flirting that had come from Jack. Of course she'd knocked him back. She was about to spend two weeks working with the man and the only relationship she wanted was a professional one, hopefully based on mutual respect and trust.

And what about that reaction to Matt being the nurse?

Lia's high spirits dimmed a little. Was it expected

to be part of the deal? Did FIFOs get paid so well because it was assumed they would provide a bonus service to men working in isolated places?

They probably did when they were working with Sam Taylor—if he was single, that was, which seemed unlikely. How many men who were that good-looking were still unattached in their midthirties, as he looked to be?

Mind you, there *was* something unusual about him. Something that didn't quite fit the picture she might have expected. Something that made him look almost as if he was here by mistake.

Not like Jack, who had the rugged good looks of a pirate and a cheekiness that suggested he liked to live on the edge, which made wanting to live in an isolated place like this quite plausible. But Sam? He looked like he was playing a role—that was it. With his sun-streaked, floppy dark blond hair and blue-grey eyes, he could easily be a film star cast as a doctor in a tropical paradise.

Intriguing.

She wasn't interested in meeting someone, she reminded herself.

But if she was, there would have been no contest between Sam and Jack, so it was probably just as well Sam hadn't shown even a glimmer of interest in her. Quite the opposite, in fact, judging by the way he'd turned his back and walked away.

'Looks like we've been abandoned.' Jack shrugged. 'Want to have a look at the helicopter before I give you the grand tour of everything else?'

'Sure.' Lia turned her head, her smile polite. 'It's a BK117, isn't it? Fully specced?'

'We've got everything your paramedic heart could desire. Even a portable ventilator and ultrasound.'

'Awesome. The only other thing I need is a pilot with exceptional skill.'

'At your service.' Jack tugged at his fringe. 'I might push the boundaries but I'm not about to risk killing myself or any of my crew.' He returned her smile. 'And, judging from your CV they sent through, you're going to be one of the best I've worked with. And…um… sorry about, you know…I'm not usually a jerk. This job is my life. Maybe I got a bit overexcited about meeting someone who has the same passion.'

He wouldn't be trying it on again, either. This time her smile was genuine. 'We're going to get along just fine, Jack.' She couldn't help turning her head to where a golf cart was sending up a cloud of dust as it carried Sam and Matt away from the airstrip. The question of how well she might be going to get on with the medical staff here was an entirely different matter.

'Are we…um…going to have a look around the hospital some time, too?'

'It's our base.' Jack nodded. 'We hang out in the staffroom on our downtime so that we're within coo-ee of the radio. You'll probably get roped in to help with some of the medical stuff, I expect. We always seem to be a bit short-staffed.'

So she'd be seeing Sam again. Probably quite a lot of him.

Not that it should matter. If anything, it should be something that could be seen as a potential conflict, given the odd vibe he'd put out.

So why were her spirits lifting again?

Because she couldn't resist a challenge? It was intriguing, that was all. She wouldn't mind finding out how he'd ended up here and why he'd stayed.

And she'd definitely like to rub his nose in that attitude to how capable a female paramedic could be.

Yep. That would be a bonus.

And Lia was very good at rising to any challenge to prove herself.

She followed Jack towards the helicopter, which was well anchored to cope with the rising wind gusts. Not that they were likely to be flying anytime soon in these conditions, but the sooner the better, as far as she was concerned.

She could feel her fingers curling into fists.

Bring it on...

CHAPTER TWO

'WHAT'S WITH THE white coat, Sam?'

'It's my doctor coat.' The grin on his favourite nurse's face was irritating. 'You get to wear a uniform every day, Ana. What's wrong with me looking a bit more professional? Besides, I never realised how useful all these pockets were. Look—I can fit my diary and phone and even my stethoscope in here…' Sam pulled some sterile gloves from the wall dispenser and shoved those in another pocket. 'I'm ready for anything.'

'You look more like you're about to front an advertisement for washing powder or something. You know…' She dropped her voice. 'Laboratory tests have proved Wonder Wash to be a thousand percent more effective than other leading brands.'

Sam snorted. 'You've changed, Ana. You used to show a bit more respect.'

The grin widened. 'Maybe it's because I'm a happily married woman now.'

He had to smile back. 'You are. And it's great. I'm really happy for you, even if you didn't invite me to the wedding.'

'Like you would have dropped everything and come all the way to London for a few days. It was hard enough persuading my mother to be there. And you'll get your wedding fix soon enough.'

'True. Is it next week that Caroline and Keanu are tying the knot?'

'The week after. Oh...who's this coming in with Jack?'

Sam turned his head. Sure enough, there were two people entering the wide walkway that linked the three wings of Wildfire hospital around its lush tropical garden. Something in the garden had clearly attracted Lia's attention and they had paused as she'd pointed. Maybe she'd spotted an exotic bird near the pond in the garden's centre. Sam found himself checking that the lapels on his white coat were sitting flat. Not that he was about to tell Ana but there was a reason he'd wanted to look particularly professional today.

'That's the new FIFO paramedic. She came in yesterday with the new nurse. Have you met Matt yet?'

'Of course. He's giving Rangi his bath.' Her lips twitched. 'It may take a while. There's a lot to wash.'

'We've got to try and get his weight down. The diabetes and skin sores are only going to be the start of his health issues.'

'Mmm. I have to say it's going to be a treat to have a male nurse on board for a while. Matt didn't even need the winch to get Rangi out of bed.' But Ana's interest was elsewhere for the moment. 'Has our new paramedic got a name?'

'Lia...something. Sounded Italian.'

'She looks Italian. And...*gorgeous*...'

It was Sam's turn to make a sound of feigned interest but he had to turn his head again. Jack and Lia were much closer now and it was no wonder Ana was impressed.

The short shorts and wild hair he remembered from the airstrip yesterday were gone. Lia was wearing long, dark cargo pants and the black T-shirt with the red emblem of Wildfire's rescue service. Her hair sat smoothly against her head with a complicated braid arrangement that went from her forehead on both sides to merge into a thick rope at the back.

She looked...professional.

'Hey, Ana. This is Lia, my new crewmate. Lia, this is Anahera Kopu, one of our permanent nurses.'

'It's Wilson now, Jack. I got married, remember?' Ana held out her hand to shake Lia's. 'You've got to show me how to do my hair like that. It's amazing.'

'It's dead easy. And...um...congratulations? I'm guessing your wedding was recent?'

'A couple of months ago. I just got back from London. And a honeymoon in Paris.'

'Wow... Two places I'd love to visit.'

'You haven't been yet?'

'Travelling's never been in my budget.' But Lia was smiling. 'That's why it's so exciting to be *here*.'

Because it was a new country or because it was adding to the reserves in her budget? The knot of tension in Sam's gut was as unfamiliar as the starched fabric of the coat sleeves on his bare arms. He started rolling the sleeves up a bit.

'We've got an outpatient clinic to get started, Ana.' He nodded at Lia. 'Has Jack got you settled in all right? Happy with your accommodation?'

'It's fantastic. I love it. I woke up this morning and

looked out at the view of the sea and all those islands and couldn't believe how beautiful it all is.'

It wasn't just her eyes that shone with pleasure—her whole face seemed to light up. It was impossible not to smile back.

'Looks better on a nice day.' He turned to Jack. 'Are you up with the forecast? How's that cyclone tracking?'

'Bit too close for comfort, this one. We could be in for a rough few days.'

'I'd better check the stocks in Emergency,' Ana said. 'We always get a rush on dressings and sutures and things in a cyclone. It's amazing the debris that people can get hit with.'

'Hettie might be able to do that when it's quiet later. She's on the afternoon shift, isn't she?'

Ana nodded. 'I'll see how many people we've got in the waiting room for the clinic, then.'

'I'd love to have a look around your emergency department,' Lia said. 'If that's okay?'

In the tiny silence that followed her query Sam realised that the question had been directed at him. If he was honest, though, he'd known that already. He could feel Lia's gaze on his skin.

'Sure.' He met her gaze long enough to be polite. 'Jack knows his way around. Feel free to explore the whole—' The sound of his telephone ringing stopped his invitation. He delved into his pocket to extract the phone from the tangle of his stethoscope and that was irritating enough to make him loop the stethoscope around his neck with one hand as he answered the call with the other.

He'd been expecting this. 'Yes, it's all sorted, Pita.' He stepped away from the others and lowered his voice.

'I'm tied up in a clinic this morning but I'll leave it beside the radio in the staffroom. White envelope with your name on it.'

He heard a burst of laughter behind him but he kept moving as he ended his call. He had work to do and he knew the waiting room would be filling up fast. He didn't have time for any social chitchat. His visit to the staffroom would not even include stopping to make a coffee.

Not that being busy was enough to explain the odd tension he was aware of. Maybe that had more to do with the fact that he could still feel Lia watching him as he walked away.

Déjà vu.

Lia watched Sam walking away. Maybe she would have to get used to feeling like she wasn't overly welcome here.

She certainly needed to get over letting it get to her. She pasted a smile on her face as she turned back to Jack and Ana, but they were looking at each other.

'What's with the white coat? Has Sam been down in the lab already this morning or something?'

Ana shook her head. 'Not that I know of.' She grinned at Jack. 'He said that he just wanted to look professional.'

Lia caught her bottom lip with her teeth to stop her saying anything. Like confessing that she had started the day in exactly the same way. The French braiding of her hair hadn't been nearly as easy as she'd implied to Ana. It had taken ages and it had been Sam she'd been thinking of as she'd stared into the mirror and tried to perfect her professional look.

Had he done the same thing with that pristine-looking coat?

And if so…why?

To impress *her*?

He was still within sight on the walkway. In fact, he'd stopped in his tracks and was staring at something outside in the garden. Lia had been entranced by the flock of rainbow-coloured parrots she'd seen earlier and had had to point them out to Jack, but he'd been far less interested because it was something he saw every day so they would be unlikely to have attracted Sam's attention, either.

'Ana?' Sam's call was calm but they could all sense the urgency. 'Grab the resus trolley, will you? I can see someone lying on the path.'

He disappeared behind the greenery of the lush shrubs hedging the walkway and Lia's reaction was automatic. As Ana raced down the walkway to vanish through a door, Lia ran in the opposite direction—to follow Sam. She could hear the rattle of trolley wheels behind her as she pushed through the hedge to where Sam was now crouched over a sprawled figure.

'Is he breathing?'

'Can't tell. Help me roll him over.'

He was a large man and it needed them both to roll him onto his back. Lia immediately tilted his head to make sure his airway was open and then she put her cheek close to his face and laid a hand on his diaphragm to feel for any air movement.

'He's not breathing.'

Sam had his fingers on the man's neck. 'There's no pulse.'

Ana had had to go further down the walkway to find

a gap to get the trolley through, and Jack was helping her, but there was no time to wait until they were there with the life pack and the bag mask. Lia already had her hands positioned in the centre of the man's chest and she began compressions without waiting for any instruction from Sam.

'I wonder how much downtime there's been already.'

'Not much, I hope. I think it was the sound of him falling that made me look over the hedge. He broke a few branches on the way down.'

She could feel Sam watching her as he spoke. Assessing her performance. Fair enough. This was a big man and it took a lot of strength to be able to make sure she was pushing hard enough to create an output from his heart. She could feel a sweat breaking out but she kept her arms straight and kept pushing. Hard and fast. At least a hundred compressions a minute, she reminded herself. And a third of the chest for their depth.

Ana threw a bag mask to Sam as she stopped the trolley. He caught it easily and in one swift movement had the mask over the man's nose and mouth. He hooked his fingers under the chin to help press hard enough to create a good seal and then flicked a glance at Lia, who paused her compressions to allow him to squeeze the bag and deliver a couple of assisted breaths. The chest rose and fell twice and she started compressions again as soon as she saw the chest falling for the second time. Her arms were aching with the effort now but she knew she couldn't slow down, even as Ana was cutting the man's T-shirt to pull it clear and sticking the defibrillator pads on the side just below his heart and beneath the collarbone on the other side.

She began counting aloud to let Sam know when it was time to deliver another breath. Jack had attached the oxygen bottle to the mask.

'Twenty-eight…twenty-nine…thirty…' She held her hands clear as another two breaths were delivered.

The static on the defibrillator screen was settling and they could all see that their patient was in the potentially fatal rhythm of ventricular fibrillation.

'Come and take over the airway,' Sam instructed Ana. 'I'll get an IV in after the first shock.'

Lia could hear the tone of the life pack charging.

'Stand clear,' Sam ordered. 'Shocking now…'

The rhythm didn't change.

'Do you need a break, Lia?' Sam was pulling IV supplies from the trolley.

'No. I'll let you know when I do.'

'You're doing a good job. I'll take over after the next shock.'

The praise was enough to banish the ache in her arms and to ignore the sting of perspiration getting into her eyes.

Clearly hampered by his white coat, Sam stripped it off and shoved it onto the bottom of the trolley. Then he moved swiftly enough to have an IV line inserted and the first dose of drugs on board before the end of the two minutes of CPR that meant another shock was due to be delivered.

'Who is he, do you know?' Jack asked.

'He's Rangi's brother, Keoni,' Ana said. 'And I think he had an outpatient appointment this morning. Sam wants to test the whole family for diabetes.'

'Stand clear,' Sam ordered again.

Lia sat back on her heels this time, ready to move

out of the way so that Sam could take over the compressions.

But this time the spike of the shock being delivered on the life-pack screen gave way to a blip of a normal beat. And then another and another.

'He's gagging,' Ana said a moment later. 'I'll take the airway out.'

'We'll need a bed,' Sam said. 'And a few extra hands to move him.'

'I'll get Matt,' Ana said, scrambling to her feet. 'And anyone else I can find. Or do you need me here, Sam?'

Sam caught Lia's gaze. 'No…you go, Ana. We're fine.'

The eye contact was only there for a moment but Lia felt like she'd passed some sort of test.

And she'd got good marks.

It was always a bonus to cheat death like this and have a successful resuscitation from a cardiac arrest but this felt even sweeter than usual. And the good marks went both ways. This success had been a team effort and Sam had shown himself to be a calm and competent leader.

'We'll get him into our intensive care unit,' Sam said. 'You may as well join us, Lia, and start your tour of the hospital with the pointy end.'

'I'll help you move him,' Jack said. 'And then maybe I should let them know that the outpatient clinic will be starting a bit late.'

'Give Keanu a call. He can come in early and get things started.' Sam was adjusting the wheel on the IV tubing to change the rate of fluids being delivered from the bag of saline he was holding up. His smile was wry. 'It looks like it's going to be another one of "those" days, all right…'

There was a gleam in his eye that suggested that those sorts of days were actually the ones he liked best and Lia found herself smiling back at him. She loved the adrenaline rush of dealing with emergencies, too. And the challenge of multi-tasking when it looked like there might be too much to handle but you knew the buzz of being able to cope was well worth the stress levels.

To be honest, smiling at Sam Taylor was no hardship. He looked so much better now that he'd discarded the formal white coat. His short-sleeved, open-necked shirt exposed tanned skin and he must have pushed his sun-streaked, floppy hair back from his forehead a few times during that intense scenario to have made it look so spiky and slightly disreputable.

And even with the wry twist to that smile, it was irresistible. What would he look like if he was really amused and those crinkles at the corners of his eyes deepened? What would his laugh sound like?

Lia suspected it would be a very contagious sound. Had her early impressions been unjustified? Maybe Sam was actually quite a nice guy. He was certainly a very good doctor and that was more than enough to chase away any doubts that she might not enjoy working here.

Extra sets of hands were arriving from all corners of the hospital and Sam had more than enough to do, co-ordinating the helpers to lift Keoni onto the bed and arrange the equipment carefully so it didn't get disconnected. He put the life pack on the bed between their patient's legs so he could keep an eye on the rhythm on the screen. The bed didn't have an IV pole attached so someone had to carry the bag of fluid high enough to keep it running. It was logical to give that task to Jack, who was the tallest person there apart from himself.

Their patient was beginning to take breaths unaided but not at a fast enough rate so he needed someone who could move alongside the bed, holding the mask in place to deliver oxygen and to assist his breathing when needed by compressing the bag attached to the mask. At any other time Sam would have asked Ana to do that because she was the most experienced nurse when it came to any protocols to do with resuscitation or post-resuscitation care. But Lia had been doing that since Ana had gone to look for extra help and she'd proved herself to be more than competent. It would be rude to push her aside and he'd invited her to come to his intensive care unit anyway.

Besides...despite how focused he was on transferring a patient who was still critical and could potentially arrest again at any moment, there was a part of his mind that was aware of appreciating Lia being there.

It wasn't due solely to the competence she'd displayed in handling an emergency situation and it certainly wasn't because of some masculine instinct that simply enjoyed having an attractive female nearby. Maybe it was his better nature asserting itself and being prepared to give her a chance to prove his first impression wrong.

Or maybe it had something to do with that smile...

'If I was at home, I'd be transporting to a facility that had a cath lab,' Lia said as they manoeuvred the bed into the walkway. 'Do you have the capacity to do angiography here?'

'No,' Ana told her. 'We've got a lot of things that remote hospitals might dream of having, like a CT scanner, but a cath lab would be taking things a bit too far.'

'So how do you treat your cardiac patients?'

'We'll take a twelve-lead ECG,' Sam responded. 'And a chest X-ray. We can check cardiac enzymes and we'll administer thrombolysis if it's indicated.'

The sound of a wolf-whistle made him blink but he ignored it.

'As soon as we've got him stable enough, we'll arrange a fixed-wing evacuation to a hospital on the mainland that can do angiography and angioplasty. Cardiac surgery, if that's what's needed.'

The wolf-whistle sounded again. Frowning, he looked up from the rhythm he was watching on the screen to see Lia reaching into the pocket of her cargo pants to pull out a mobile phone.

What the heck? Okay, she was still holding the patient's mask in place with one hand but how inappropriate could you get? Had she even been listening to the response to her query?

She was actually texting as she stepped back to let the hospital staff position the bed and hook up the equipment they now had available. Any impression he'd had of Lia's competence and professionalism was beginning to fade and maybe that was why he gave her the challenge of interpreting the ECG trace as soon as he'd put the chest leads on and printed it off.

He stepped close enough to hold the sheet of graph paper in front of her. 'So what do you think?'

Lia jumped and her gaze jerked up from her phone

but she still had it clutched in her hand as she turned her attention to the trace.

Her scanning was as rapid as his had been.

'Hyperacute T waves, and there's significant ST elevation in leads V3 to V5. Looks like a sizeable anterior infarction with lateral extension.'

He wanted to test her. 'What about the bundle branch block?'

'There is a left bundle branch block but the ST elevation is greater than you'd expect and we've got Q waves here…and here…'

He hadn't noticed how delicate her fingers were before. Long and slim, with practical, unpainted nails and no rings. Her touch on the paper was light enough not to move it but he could feel the pressure transfer itself to his own fingertips.

'And there's some reciprocal changes in the inferior leads,' Lia added. 'It's pretty conclusive.'

He should have been impressed. He might have even told her that except for the interruption of that damned wolf-whistle again.

Her cheeks went pink. 'Oops, sorry. I meant to put that on silent.'

Sam glared at her. 'Maybe you could save your personal messaging for out of work hours.'

'I've got the bloods done.' Ana had a handful of test tubes. 'Some will have to go down to the lab but do you want me to do the benchtop cardiac biomarkers?'

'I'll do it.' Sam turned away from Lia. 'Set up the tenecteplase infusion, will you? And draw up some atropine. I'm not happy with his rate. It's sinus but it's too slow.'

A glance from the corner of his eye as he transferred

some blood to the tiny, specialised tube that would slot into the sophisticated device he was now holding in his hand showed Sam that Lia was busy texting again. Maybe she already knew that they could measure things like troponin and creatinine kinase and myoglobin, which were all markers of whether someone was having a heart attack and how large it was, but surely she should be interested to know that she would have one of these units available in the helicopter she was about to start working in?

They hadn't been cheap but, like a fair few other items here, they were important enough for Sam to have quietly provided them from his personal funds.

Not something he would want Lia—or others, for that matter—to know. Maybe it was better that she wasn't showing any interest or asking awkward questions.

And at least she put her damned phone away when Jack's pager sounded an alert.

'Looks like we've got a call. Come on, Lia. I'll show you how the radio system works.'

'Holy heck…' The straps of her harness tightened to hold Lia in the front seat of the helicopter as it fought the wind. 'How far have we got to go?'

'Only another five minutes.' Jack's voice was reassuringly calm inside her helmet but the sidelong glance he gave her was more concerned. 'These *are* pretty marginal flying conditions. You okay?'

'Are you kidding?' Lia laughed aloud as they slewed sideways and rocked again. 'I *love* it.'

The look she got now was impressed. 'I've had a few guys in that seat who'd have white knuckles by now.'

'How will we get to patients if it gets any worse than this? Do you think the cyclone's going to be a direct hit?'

'It's looking more likely. We might well have a day or two when we can't get airborne. If that's the case, we use boats for the closer islands. How do you go in rough seas?'

Lia grinned. 'I quite like them, too.'

Jack shook his head, silent for a moment as he focused on controlling his helicopter. The main island of Atangi was within sight now and Lia could see that it was far more populated than Wildfire. Somewhere in that cluster of buildings was the medical centre they were heading for after getting a call from the nurse who was working there.

'I used to ride horses way back,' Lia said. 'What I loved most was a good cross-country course. Boats and aircraft in a bit of rough stuff is like competing in cross-country when you never know where the next jump is or how big it's going to be.'

'You still ride?'

'No. It's not exactly an affordable hobby. Besides…' Lia let out a whoop as they were buffeted by some particularly big turbulence. 'I get all the excitement I need these days from my job.'

'Yeah…' Jack was clearly in complete agreement. 'Let's get this baby on the ground and hope that our patient doesn't get airsick on the way back. If she does, it's your job to clean up.'

'Don't think so, mate.' Lia was still grinning. 'It's *your* helicopter.'

CHAPTER THREE

THE MEDICAL CLINIC on Atangi was staffed by an older local nurse, Marnie, who met them at the door after Jack had landed the helicopter on the football field across the road. He shut the chopper down and came with her in case he needed to go back for a stretcher.

'Try not to scare her,' Marnie warned. 'I had a hard job persuading her to come in at all and she might try and do a runner. Not that she'll get very far, mind you…'

'What's her name?' Lia asked. 'And what's the story?'

'Her name's Sefina. She lives out past the edge of the village and keeps to herself, of course…'

Of course? A warning bell rang for Lia. She wanted to ask why it was expected that this Sefina would keep to herself but the nurse was still speaking quietly.

'I went out there on my way home for lunch because she missed her appointment for Joni's fifteen-month vaccinations last week and I wanted to remind her how important it was that she brings him in.'

'Joni?'

'Her kid. Anyway, when she finally answered the door, it was obvious something bad had happened. She said she had a fall on the rocks at the beach yesterday but…'

Lia touched her arm to slow their progress towards the consulting room. She needed to ask this time.

'But what?'

'Everyone knows what her husband, Louis, can be like after a few drinks,' Jack muttered. 'Is that what you're thinking, Marnie?'

The older woman shrugged and looked away. 'It's none of my business,' she said. 'I only went there because of Joni…'

Lia raised her eyebrows at Jack. What on earth was going on here? This was a village and surely everybody knew everybody else's business—and looked out for them?

'It's a long story,' Jack said quietly. 'I'll fill you in later.'

Sitting in the middle of the consulting-room floor was a small boy with coffee-coloured skin and a mop of wild curls. At the sight of strangers entering the room, his face crumpled and he let out a wail of fear and made a beeline for his mother's legs for something to cling to.

The boy's mother couldn't help, however, because she was currently vomiting into the handbasin at one side of the room.

Lia went swiftly to her side.

'Sefina? I'm Lia. I've come to help you.'

Her patient looked up as she turned the tap on and Lia was shocked by the injury to her face. One eye was so swollen it was closed and there was a cut above it that needed suturing. And even on Sefina's dark skin the bruising around the cut was obvious. She was also shocked at how young she was. Barely more than a teenager, by the look of it, and she was a mother already.

'I'm fine. I didn't want to come in here…Marnie shouldn't have called you.'

'I know.' Lia kept her smile as reassuring as her tone. 'But we're here now so let me give you a check-up? I'm new in this job so I have to make sure everything's done properly. You're my first patient, even.'

She wanted to let Sefina know that she didn't know anything about whatever it was that was keeping this young woman isolated from her community and that she was offering treatment without any kind of judgement. She wasn't going to be fobbed off, however. She'd seen more than a tinge of blood in that basin before the tap had been turned on and that was a red flag for injuries that could be internal.

'Marnie shouldn't have called you. I'm fine.'

The repetition of something that had just been said rang another warning bell for Lia. The head injury was clearly enough to have caused concussion or possibly a more serious brain injury.

'Do you know what day it is today, Sefina?'

'Marnie shouldn't have called you.' Sefina had turned away from the basin. 'Joni… Come on…we're going home…'

She started to bend over to pick up her son, who was still clinging to her legs, but then she clutched her abdomen and doubled over with a cry of pain.

Supporting her weight, Lia had to let her slide to the floor when it became obvious she couldn't get as far as the bed. Whatever this girl's injuries were, they needed more investigation than it was likely to be possible to do in this small clinic.

'Jack?' Lia knew he was waiting right outside the door and, sure enough, he appeared instantly.

'We're going to need the stretcher,' she told him. 'I don't think Sefina's going to be walking anywhere just now.'

It was impossible to start examining Sefina with Joni now trying to scramble into her arms. Lia lifted the toddler and turned to find Marnie watching, her arms folded over her ample chest.

'Can you look after Joni, please, Marnie? I need to examine Sefina.'

'*No-o-o...*' Sefina struggled to sit up but fell back with a cry of pain.

The hesitation and then grudging compliance from the nurse was enough to anger Lia. Whatever the village had against this young girl, it was not acceptable to be taking it out on an innocent child. By the time Jack returned, Lia was tight-lipped. She met him in the waiting room.

'We have to get Sefina back to the hospital. Her abdomen's rigid and I suspect she's bleeding from a ruptured spleen. On top of that she's got a head injury and there's no way of telling how serious it is. She needs a CT scan to rule out a brain bleed.'

Jack was nodding. 'Let's go, then.'

'There's another thing,' Lia snapped. 'I'm not leaving her baby here. I think there's a high chance these injuries weren't accidental. There's no way I'm letting that little boy go back to his father and I'm getting the feeling that no one else around here wants to take care of him.'

'Louis isn't his father,' Jack told her.

Lia blinked. Was that what the problem was? Had Sefina cheated on her husband and everyone knew that? Did her low-life husband think it gave him an excuse to beat her up to within an inch of her life?

'All the more reason to take Joni with us, then.'

'It'll be a rough flight.'

'So we'll strap him in. Or I'll hold him. There's not much I can do for Sefina en route, anyway. I'll give her some pain relief and get some fluids up and then what we need to do is get her to hospital as soon as possible. Hopefully before this weather gets any worse.'

Sam, Hettie and Anahera were waiting in the emergency department of Wildfire Island's hospital, having been alerted to the incoming trauma patient via radio.

Jack and Manu, the hospital porter, were wheeling the stretcher. Lia had her arms full with a very frightened-looking small child. Sam had heard of the child, of course. Everybody in this community had. But he'd never seen him. Or his mother, for that matter. Good grief, she looked *so* young...

'Let's get her onto the bed.' Sam positioned himself at the head. 'On the count of three. One, two...three...'

Sefina was transferred smoothly from the stretcher to the bed. Lia moved closer to Sam but still had to raise her voice over the crying of the child she was holding.

'This is Sefina Dason,' Lia said. 'She's sustained head and abdominal trauma. GCS is down at fourteen. Repetitive speech and vomiting. Her abdo's rigid and her blood pressure is low at one hundred over forty. Up from ninety over forty after a litre of saline. She's in sinus rhythm and tachycardic at one-three-five, and has a resp rate of thirty. Her oxygen saturation was ninety-five per cent. It's come up to ninety-eight on oxygen. She's had ten milligrams of morphine. Provisional diagnosis is a ruptured spleen and concussion.'

Anahera was changing the oxygen tubing from the portable cylinder to the overhead port. Hettie was wrapping a blood-pressure cuff around Sefina's arm.

'Mechanism of injury?' Sam queried.

'Apparently a fall onto rocks.'

Sam raised an eyebrow at her tone as he stepped closer to Lia to take the patient report form she was holding. Glancing down at her notes, he saw the question mark in front of the words 'non-accidental injury'.

It was a serious accusation to make. He met Lia's gaze and she stared back. He could see anger in her eyes. She started to say something quietly but he couldn't hear over the noise the child was making.

'Is he injured, too?'

'Not that I'm aware of.'

'So why did you bring him? Surely there was a family member or friend who could have cared for him?'

Hettie was reaching up to hook the bag of IV fluids onto the pole at the head of the bed. She turned and her gaze was clearly caught by the sight of the scared toddler. Sam could see the way her face creased into lines of sympathy as her heart went out to the child.

'I'll take him,' she said, 'while you finish your handover.' She scooped Joni into her arms and walked away. 'He might be hungry. I'll go and see if Vailea's got something in the kitchen. Like ice cream, maybe.' She was cuddling the baby close to her body. 'Do you like ice cream, sweetheart?'

Sefina didn't seem to have noticed that her child was being taken from the room. She was drowsy from the morphine. Or maybe the head injury.

'Get another set of vitals, please, Ana. And check that her GCS hasn't dropped. I'll do an ultrasound on her belly.'

As he turned to find the equipment he needed he found himself the subject of an icy glare from Lia. She stepped away from the bed with a head tilt that summoned Sam to mirror her movements.

'Take a look at your patient,' she said, her voice quiet but fierce. 'You'll find welts on her abdomen that look like marks from the sole of a boot. Would you have left a child in the care of someone who could do that?'

'Of course not.' The tension in the air between them was enough that a small thing could ignite it, but this time it had nothing to do with Lia's looks or personality. They were both on the same side here. Sam could feel anger forming an unpleasant knot in his gut but, weirdly, there was something good to be found, as well. It felt good to have Lia on his side. As if, together, they made up a force to be reckoned with.

'Have the police been informed?'

'Not yet. I don't know what your protocols are and, anyway, the priority was to get Sefina here.'

With a nod, Sam turned back to his patient. Lia was right—they needed to work fast. As soon as he was happy that Sefina was stable, they would get a CT scan done if it was indicated and go from there, as far as her treatment went. Right now, it looked as if emergency surgery could well be part of that treatment. The full story, and any repercussions from it, would have to wait.

They were one staff member down, with Hettie having taken Joni away. 'Can you stay?' Sam asked Lia. 'We might need a hand.'

She glanced at Jack, who was manoeuvring the stretcher away. 'You may as well,' he said. 'I'm going to go back and make sure the helicopter's locked down. We won't be flying anywhere else for a while. We were lucky to get back here.' He gave Sam a wry smile. 'It was a wild ride,' he added. 'And I've never seen anyone cope as well as Lia did.'

Sam had been in a few rough helicopter rides himself. He knew how difficult it could be to try and manage a patient in those conditions. He also knew that it could be downright scary. No wonder there was such a note of admiration in Jack's voice. It shouldn't be irritating.

Maybe it was just another coal on the fire of the anger that sprang from a man hurting a woman, if that really was what had happened to Sefina. He needed to protect his patient. And maybe he wanted to protect Lia, too, from the kind of casual relationships he knew the pilot enjoyed. He'd had more than one woman in the past crying on his shoulder because they'd believed they could be the one who changed Jack's mind about being a bachelor.

The thought of Lia crying on his shoulder was strangely appealing for a moment. But it was also ridiculous and he shook it off as he began his examination of their patient. Lia could look after herself. In fact, she could probably cope with anything, and if she did hook up with Jack, it would be more likely to be their pilot who'd be crying on Sam's shoulder. The thought brought a faint curl to the corners of his mouth but they vanished as he focused on his patient.

'Let's get another line in and some more fluids up. Type and crossmatch in case we need a blood transfusion. Sefina? Open your eyes, love. Do you know where you are?'

Sefina moaned but did open her eyes. Sam could see the moment she was awake enough to be frightened again and it was heartbreaking to see how very scared she was.

'It's okay,' he told her. 'You're in the hospital, love. We're going to take care of you. You're safe now…'

Sefina rolled her head to one side and then the other.

'Joni… Where's Joni?' She was trying to sit up now. One of the electrodes that was monitoring her heart rhythm popped off her arm and an alarm began to sound.

Lia caught the dangling wire and snapped the electrode back onto the sticky dot. She had her face close to Sefina's and she caught the girl's hand in her own and held it.

'He's fine, Sefina. We're taking care of him, too.'

'Where am I?'

'You're in the hospital. I'm Lia, remember? I came to see you at the clinic. We brought you in here because you're hurt and now you're safe. And Joni's safe.'

Her voice was calm and even Sam was starting to feel the tension ebb. And that *smile*… 'I promise…'

Tears were rolling down Sefina's cheeks but she nodded slowly.

'It *hurts*,' she whispered. 'My tummy hurts…'

'I know. We're going to find out why and then we'll fix it, okay?'

Sam's glance, he hoped, thanked Lia for making this easier before he made eye contact with Sefina. The girl was still clutching Lia's hand but a lot of that fear had gone.

'I'm Sam,' he told her gently. 'One of the doctors here. Is it okay if I have a look at your tummy now?'

It was Lia the girl looked towards for reassurance before she nodded again. It was Lia's hand she had to hold whenever it was possible during the barrage of tests they employed to find out exactly how serious Sefina's injuries were.

It was more than an hour later when they could review all the results.

'There's no bleeding in her head. That's a bonus.'

'Definite concussion, though. She's still vomiting and she's very drowsy.' Anahera glanced over her shoulder to where Sefina was sleeping, now receiving a transfusion to counteract the amount of blood she was losing internally. 'I still need to suture that head laceration. Unless you want to do it?'

'Let's do it in Theatre.' Sam looked at Lia. 'Your provisional diagnosis was spot-on. She's still bleeding from the rupture to her spleen. We'll have to take it out.'

'You can do that here?'

'We can't do anything else. There's no way we can evacuate her in this weather. We weren't even able to send off our man who had the arrest this morning. We'll be keeping him here for a few days, by the look of things. Anyway, it was lucky that you and Jack could get her here so fast. A boat trip could have made things a whole lot worse.'

'Anything I can do to help?'

'Maybe go and see what's happening with the little boy. I'll need Hettie in Theatre. Do you know where the kitchens are?'

'I'll find them.'

As she went through the doorway, Sam saw her slip her hand into her pocket and take out her phone. Had it been vibrating silently even as Lia had been assisting them with this emergency?

And he'd felt the need to protect her from Jack? Irritation bubbled out.

'Hurry up,' he called after her. 'It would be better if you could attend to your love-life later.'

Love-life?

As if…

A nurse pointed Lia in the direction of the kitchens and she sped along the walkway. The windows had been shuttered against the wind and they rattled and shook with a disturbing ferocity. There was no rain yet but it wasn't far away.

She found Hettie in the kitchen, spooning ice cream into Joni's mouth. She got to her feet instantly when Lia passed on the message that she was needed in Theatre and she bent to kiss the toddler as she gave a swift farewell to the older woman working at the bench.

Lia smiled at her. 'Hi…I'm Lia.'

'I know.' The woman's smile was friendly. 'I'm Vailea. I'm in charge of the kitchens here. Can I get you a cup of tea or something?'

'That would be great—if you've got time.'

'I've got plenty of help, as you can see.' A wave of her hand took in the small group of island girls in their white aprons and caps. 'Moana? Take Joni through to the ward, will you? Ask one of the nurses to find a nappy and help you change him. And ask if they've got a spare cot. I think he might need a sleep.'

The tea was strong and sweet, just the way Lia liked it. She also liked it that Vailea came to sit at the big table with her to have her own drink.

'Sefina's going to be in hospital for a few days at least. Do you know what will happen with Joni? Will they keep him in here with her?'

'Probably. I'll have a word with my daughter later when they're not so busy. You've met Anahera?'

'Yes…is she your daughter?'

Vailea nodded. 'And she has a daughter, as well. Hana. A bit older than Joni but we're well used to looking after little ones. I might end up taking him home with me for a few days. Poor wee mite…'

Lia sipped her tea thoughtfully. Her curiosity about her first patient here on the islands was strong enough to make her push the boundaries of patient confidentiality. Vailea obviously knew enough to make her feel sorry for Joni.

She bit her lip but then raised her gaze. 'Jack said that Sefina's husband isn't Joni's father…'

Vailea's glance was sharp. Was it telling her that this was none of her business? Except it was, kind of…

'I got the feeling that she might need help. That…um…other people might need to be called in.'

Valiea clicked her tongue. 'Did that no-good Louis do this to her?' She shook her head sadly. 'It was never going to work…'

'What wasn't?'

'The arrangement.'

Lia stayed silent but her face must have advertised her confusion.

Vailea sighed. 'Joni is the son of Ian Lockhart. The family that owns Wildfire and started the gold mine way back. They're mostly good people. Max Lockhart is the one who got this hospital set up to provide for all the islanders. And his daughter, Caroline, is one of our best nurses. But Ian…well, a lot of families have a black sheep, don't they?'

Lia nodded. It sounded like this Lockhart family was the equivalent of royalty on these islands and that kind of power could be used to devastating effect by someone who lacked scruples.

'Everybody knows the story so I don't see why you shouldn't,' Vailea continued. 'It didn't surprise anyone that Ian got Sefina pregnant. What did surprise us was that he brought her back here from Fiji after her family threw her out. Not that he intended to ever marry her himself, of course. No…he hired Louis to do that because everybody knows how lazy he is and that he'd do anything for money.'

'He paid Louis to marry her?'

'Not only that. He kept paying him. Every month. Except…'

Lia's eyebrows were about as high as they could go.

'The money ran out a while back. Ian's disappeared. Nobody knows where he is. The mine got run-down and we ended up with a collapse that killed people. There's no money even for things like spraying for mosquitoes and we've lost people to encephalitis because of it.' She shook her head. 'Everybody hates Ian so nobody wants anything to do with that poor little boy. Or his mother. And Louis…well, he's like the black sheep of the village, I guess.' Vailea was scowling now. 'But if he's done something to hurt her, something will have to be done.'

Lia nodded. 'I've told Sam. I imagine he'll call the police when they've finished the surgery. Maybe he's done it already. You do have police here, don't you?'

'Of course we do.'

Oh, dear…had she caused offence? 'Sorry…I don't know enough yet. I mean, if you have police, you need to have courts and jails and things, too, don't you?'

'There's a jail on Atangi. But if a case is serious enough it does get sent to the mainland.' Vailea reached for Lia's empty tea cup but she was smiling as she stood up. 'You'll learn about us fast enough. And I hope you'll come back. It sounds like you did a very good job today.'

Wow. Word travelled fast around these parts but it was the kind of bush telegraph Lia would have expected in a small community. What had been shocking was to learn about a darker side, where a young mother and her baby could be shut off from any support.

'I'd better get on with the dinners,' Vailea said. 'And check up on what's happening with Joni.'

'And I'd better…' Lia hesitated. What was she expected to do if the weather was too bad to fly? Did she need to wait in the staffroom near the radio in case a call came in and she needed to respond by boat? 'I'd better find Jack.'

'He'll probably be in the staffroom, if he's back from the airfield. That's where he usually hangs out.'

The shutters were still rattling as Lia made her way back along the walkway but it wasn't disturbing anymore—it was exhilarating.

Lia loved a good storm. Something wild and unpredictable and exciting. And it had been a good day today. Her first case and she'd managed it well under difficult conditions. And Sefina would be okay. They could lock her beast of a husband up in the jail and keep her safe and surely, after this, things would change.

Maybe her family back in Fiji would have a change of heart after this appalling evidence of how awful her life was here and they would take her home.

At least Joni would be well cared for over the next few days. Vailea, Anahera and especially Hettie would see to that.

Even better, she'd received word that Nico's surgery had gone well and she could let go of the guilt of not being there for him today.

Yes. It had been a very good start to her working time here. The only thing that might make the day even better was to get out into that wind for a bit. Preferably on a beach so that she would get the sting of salt water on her cheeks. And she could let the wind whip her hair and buffet her body and make her feel so alive she would have to throw her arms wide and spin around and laugh out loud with the joy of it all.

If Jack said it was okay, that was exactly what Lia intended to do.

CHAPTER FOUR

WAS SHE COMPLETELY CRAZY?

There she was, standing on the beach with big waves crashing over the coral reef and then rolling towards her in a sea of foam, probably getting soaked by the spray being picked up by the fierce wind gusts. The trees bordering the beach were bent over as if in pain and, even from this distance, Sam could hear the crack of branches about to be torn free.

And she was standing in the middle of it.

No. Not standing. She had her arms wide out to each side, like a child pretending to be an aeroplane, and she was spinning in a slow circle. Her face was tipped up and her eyes were closed and…yes…she had to be laughing, even though he couldn't hear the sound over the roar of the wind.

And then a particularly strong gust of wind knocked her off balance and Lia went sprawling onto the sand. She was struggling to get back to her feet by the time Sam reached her and she seemed happy enough to accept the offer of his hand to haul her back up.

'Isn't this amazing?' she shouted. 'I love it.'

'You're nuts,' Sam told her. 'You do realise there

are coconut palms amongst those trees and if one fell on your head it would be lights out. Probably forever.'

'I'm nowhere near the trees.'

'Branches can go a long way. And you've still got to get back up the track to get home.'

Her cheeks were bright pink from the chill of the wind mixed with sea spray. Her hair had been pulled loose from that tight arrangement of braids she'd started the day with and she looked like she hadn't been near a hairbrush in days. But her eyes were glowing with joy and that smile was wide enough to fence him in.

'You love it, too. Admit it. It's why you came down to the beach.'

'I came down to get you, you idiot. I couldn't believe it when Jack told me you'd decided to go out in this.'

But Sam was grinning now, too. She was wild, this woman. A naughty child in a grown-up's body. The sea spray had soaked her shirt and the wind had it plastered against her body. Oh, yeah…it was a very grown-up body, all right…

'He said he reckoned I could look after myself. And that he'd call me on my phone if I was needed.'

They were still having to shout to be heard over the wind. 'You think you'd even hear it?'

'It's on vibrate. I'd feel it.' Lia put her hand over the breast pocket of her shirt and Sam could see the rectangular outline of the mobile phone. How come he hadn't noticed that before when he was so aware of the way her shirt was sticking to her skin?

Because he'd been blinded by the sheer attractiveness of this woman, that's why. Something he didn't do.

The reminder of her unprofessional attention to her

phone all day was enough of a slap to bring him back to his senses.

He shook his head. 'Should have known you'd have it close. You wouldn't want to miss another text from the boyfriend.'

'What?' The smile had gone from Lia's face. The glow of exhilaration from being out in the elements had faded from her eyes, as well. 'What makes you so sure I've got a boyfriend? And when, exactly, did it become any of your business?'

'When it started interfering with how you do your job.' It was quite satisfying having to shout over the wind now. And it was good to get rid of that niggle of irritation he'd had all day. 'Every time I've seen you today, you've been fiddling with your phone.'

'And you assume that I'd let my personal life stop me doing my job properly?' Lia turned and took a step away from him. But then she turned back, almost stumbling as a wind gust caught her. 'Okay… I admit I was on the phone too much. My younger brother had surgery this morning for testicular cancer and I needed to know that he'd come through it.'

Were they tears on Lia's cheeks or was it the sea spray she was wiping away?

'I should have been there for him. I felt bad that I'd let him persuade me it was okay to come because of…of…'

The money.

That reminder should have been enough to clear his head completely of the insane attraction he was feeling towards this woman.

But there was a tiny voice in his head saying something along the lines that at least she was prepared to work for the money and not get someone else's by pretending to love them enough to score a marriage.

And she had been working. And doing a damn good job, too. If it hadn't been for her they might not have got Sefina into hospital in time.

And she was crying. She was upset because she hadn't been there for her brother and that told him something about her loyalty to the people she loved.

And maybe fate was giving things a bit of a shove. The way the wind was shoving Lia so hard she had to take a big step towards him, which knocked her off balance enough to end up bumping into him.

What was a man to do other than put his arms around her?

'I'm sorry,' he shouted. 'You should have told me. About your brother.'

'I'm sorry, too. I knew I shouldn't have been taking texts at work.'

'It didn't stop you doing your job. You were great today, Lia.'

She looked up at him, her gaze intent. 'Is Sefina okay? How did the surgery go?'

'She's fine. We took her spleen out and stopped the bleeding. She'll need a few days to get over that and the concussion but she'll be fine.'

'Has she changed her story about how it happened?'

'No. But I've had a word with our police chief, Ky. He's onto it. It's okay. I'll make sure she's safe.'

Lia was nodding. Was she actually aware that he still had his arms around her?

'And I'm sure you're brother's going to be fine, too. The survival rate for testicular cancer is great.'

She kept nodding. 'I know...'

She was still looking up at him and a new smile broke through the lines of concern for others. A relieved smile. One that underlined her apology to him and accepted his apology to her, along with the praise about her work.

It was the smile that was his undoing. On top of those huge, dark eyes that were still locked on his face. Or maybe it was the feel of her body within his arms.

Whatever…

Sam was about to do something he never did. Break a rule that was set in steel. The pull was just too strong but at least he hesitated. Made it obvious enough that Lia could stop it happening if she wanted to.

She must be more than capable of ducking a kiss that wasn't welcome…

Maybe it was because of the relief of knowing that Nico had come through his surgery and it had gone so well. She could let go of the anxiety that had been making her so tense, along with the guilt that would have haunted her forever if things hadn't gone well today.

Or maybe it was because Lia was standing in the beginnings of what was going to be a dramatic storm and the thrill of the potential danger was singing in her veins.

And maybe—if she was going to be really honest—it was because she was in the arms of a man she was already attracted to, more than she could remember ever having been attracted to any man before.

It didn't matter whether it was any or all of those reasons because Lia wasn't about to stop and analyse what was happening.

Sam Taylor was about to kiss her and she'd never wanted to *be* kissed this much.

She could feel his arms tighten around her, holding her steady in the gusts of a wind that was more than capable of knocking her off her feet again. Could taste the salt of the sea spray on his lips. Could feel the beat of his heart through clothing that was so glued to her skin now, she felt almost naked.

For a heartbeat, that was all it was. A nice kiss.

And then something changed. Something huge got unleashed and it felt bigger than the crash of the angry sea beside them and the howl of wind all around.

If this was lust, it was unlike anything Lia had ever experienced.

The warmth of this kiss was sending tendrils of fire into every cell of her body and Lia was quite sure she would never feel cold again. The silken touch of his tongue melted her bones and made her groan with the sheer ecstasy of the sensation. The sound was lost in Sam's mouth but maybe he felt it because he pulled back.

'Not here,' he said.

Her first reaction was almost fear. He was going to stop kissing her? Stop touching her? The disappointment—or maybe frustration—would be overwhelming.

'Where?'

Had she spoken the word aloud or simply let it be written all over her face?

'Come with me.'

He held her hand but it wasn't enough as the wind pushed and then pulled at her body as she tried to step over some driftwood, so he wrapped his arm around her waist and held her against his own body. A particularly big wave began its curl and descent into foam and the shower of spray was dense enough to sting their eyes and soak them both to the skin.

But they were both laughing. Fighting the elements together and loving the excitement of it. Anticipation of a very different kind of excitement was part of it, as well, and Lia could feel it sizzling and spreading from every point where Sam's body was in contact with her own.

And then they were away from the spray and protected a little from the wind as they left the beach and began climbing back up the path that Lia had used to come down to the beach from the hospital. Sam's hand gripping hers was enough to keep her steady now but he was moving fast up the track through the trees and she could hear the snap of branches and the thud of large objects hitting the ground nearby. Lia was too out of breath to say anything because she would still have to shout to be heard and…she wouldn't have known what to say, anyway.

Where was Sam taking her?

Back to the safety of the hospital? That was probably sensible, given that the sky had darkened so much it felt like night was about to fall hours too early and the first, fat drops of rain were beginning to fall. But there would be other people around at the hospital and that would be a guarantee that nothing more would happen between them. Or was he taking her to her own accommodation? That wasn't exactly private, either, with only thin walls between her room and that of other staff members, so it would end up being exactly the same dead end.

She didn't want that.

Even with the time she now had to consider whether this was a good idea or not, Lia felt no different than how she had the moment Sam had interrupted that passionate kiss.

She wanted this.

She wanted *him…*

'My house,' Sam finally shouted. 'On the end. Here…'

It was a small structure, not unlike the cluster of buildings closer to the hospital that housed both permanent and FIFO staff, but it was on its own and screened by shrubbery that was currently shedding big, glossy leaves and flowers as an offering to the rising wind. Sam had to let go of her hand to pull the door open against the force of it and then he let it shut with a bang the moment Lia had stumbled inside.

They were both out of breath and for a long, long moment they both stood there panting, their gazes locked on each other.

This was the moment. Either or both of them could admit that this might not be a good idea. That it might cause problems with them having to work together for the next couple of weeks. That they barely knew each other and they were both old enough to know that reckless physical encounters like this were something they should have grown out of long ago.

But whatever extraordinary thing had been unleashed between them was getting bigger. Gaining a momentum that Lia knew she didn't have the faintest chance of resisting. And she saw the moment that Sam realised the same thing. Heard the sound that was both an admission of defeat and an expression of a desire that echoed her own.

And then she was in his arms again and his lips were on hers and nothing else mattered. Her back was pressed against the door and she could feel her sodden clothing being peeled from her body. Her skin had to be cold because the touch of Sam's hands was far too hot to be natural and she had never felt anything like the softness of the bed she found herself on moments later.

Sex had never been like this before.

Ever…

Everything about Lia was extraordinary. Those long, lean limbs and gorgeous, firm breasts. That wild mane of dark hair that had somehow come loose from those braids so that he could wind it around his hands to hold her head in exactly the right position to capture those sweet lips.

The most extraordinary thing had to be the way she responded to every touch or sound he made, however. Instead of a normal focus on a satisfying climax for both parties, Sam found himself trying to slow things down and make it last as long as humanly possible. But this chemistry, or whatever it was, was too powerful to be tamed. With the background of the rain now hammering on the tin roof of his quarters and wooden shutters beating a tattoo in the fierce wind, it seemed as if the passion between them was a part of the elemental forces outside. It also seemed like it was over too soon.

Way too soon.

But that was okay. As they lay there closely entwined he wasn't sure where his body ended and Lia's began. Sam knew, beyond a shadow of a doubt, that this wouldn't be the only time. They had a whole two weeks to play with, and if Lia had enjoyed this encounter as much as her response suggested that she had, she would undoubtedly be just as keen as he was to make the most of every day of that two weeks. Or every night, at least.

His lips curled into a slow and very satisfied smile as he drew his head back far enough to see Lia's face.

'Wow…'

There were no words available but it didn't seem to matter because Lia was smiling, too.

'Couldn't have put it better myself.'

Her words were almost inaudible due to the sudden increase in the tropical downpour hitting the roof and her eyes widened.

'The worst of it will probably be over before too long. By tomorrow morning, maybe, with a bit of luck.'

'How will anyone get to the hospital if they need help?'

'They won't. Not unless they can get up from the village here on Wildfire. You and Jack won't be flying anywhere and I don't think any boats would manage the sea the way it'll be for a while. We'll all have to sit tight until it starts dying down. And then I expect we could be in for a busy time. It might take days to check the outlying islands.'

The faint sound of splintering glass could be heard, along with the crack of a shutter being torn free. Sam felt the sudden tension in Lia's body.

'You're safe,' he told her. 'I'll keep you safe.'

Good grief…where had that come from? Not just the words, which had seemed kind of corny the moment they had left his lips, but the sudden conviction that honouring those words was the most important thing in the world to him.

This wasn't part of the plan.

But, then, none of this had been part of any plan, had it?

The tension was contagious. Sam rolled away from Lia. 'I'd better check what that was. And maybe we should get back to the hospital and see if everything's okay.'

That's probably where he should have stayed. What had he been thinking? It was understandable that he'd gone after Lia when he'd heard that she'd been stupid enough to go to the beach as the cyclone hit, but to be hiding away in his quarters having *sex* at a time like this?

Nobody would expect behaviour like this from him. He couldn't quite believe it himself, now that the post-coital glow was wearing off. Never mind that he'd been due a break after a hectic day that had included emergency surgery. He had patients who might need him—like Sefina. He had colleagues who needed to be sure they could depend on him at all times, and especially in the potential disaster that a cyclone could bring. It might be just beginning but he'd been AWOL and that was unacceptable.

As unacceptable as hooking up with a temporary staff member?

His feet hit the floor. 'I'll find you some dry clothes.'

'How far is it from here to the hospital?'

'About two minutes, if we run.'

'I wouldn't bother about the dry clothes, then. I'd be just as wet by the time we get there.'

Knowing that Lia was planning to come with him somehow made things better. More professional, in a weird way. They couldn't change what had just happened between them, but they could put it aside and go back to how they'd been before. Two people who could work together as a team, focusing on others rather than themselves. And having those others around to dilute this disturbing attraction between them would make that so much easier.

Sam already knew how good Lia was at her job. Those skills could well be very necessary around here in the next couple of days.

'So it was worth it, then?'

'Sorry?' Lia knew she must look like a drowned rat, standing there in her sodden clothes with her hair loose and dripping down her back. No wonder everybody in the unexpectedly crowded staffroom was staring at her, but why was Jack grinning as if he knew exactly what she'd been up to?

She didn't dare turn her head to look at Sam.

'Going down to the beach to see what a cyclone looks like. It was worth getting so wet for?'

'Oh…' Maybe everybody thought that the only story here was that Sam had gone down to the beach and brought her straight back here to safety. Lia's smile was probably wider than it needed to be. 'Yes… It was… it was…amazing…'

'It was stupid, that's what it was.' Sam's voice was a growl behind her. 'I'm going to find some dry scrubs in a minute. Fill me in, Jack.' He gestured towards the radio on the desk at which the pilot was sitting. 'Any news of how things are shaping up?'

Anahera was using sign language to offer Lia a hot drink as Sam was talking to Jack. Lia smiled but shook her head. Then she smiled at Hettie, who was sitting beside Anahera, holding a sleepy-looking toddler in her lap. Seeing Joni made her want to ask about his mother's condition but she didn't want to interrupt Jack.

'The northern end of Atangi seems to be getting the worst of it so far. Mobile phone coverage is out but we've got radio contact for the moment—at least with Atangi. Ky's using the school hall on Atangi as a refuge centre and a lot of families are gathering there. No word on any of the outer islands.'

'Any boats still out?'

'Hope not. Anybody with any sense would have stopped fishing a long time ago. I did see a couple of boats heading back to port when we were flying back in from Atangi earlier. Want me to check on *your* baby?'

His *baby*? Lia had to turn her head this time—a swift, startled movement. More like a horrified one, in fact. Sam had a baby? Had she just had the most amazing sex in her life with a man who had a child, and presumably a girlfriend if not a wife, tucked away somewhere?

Jack saw her expression and laughed. 'I'm talking about his yacht. *Surf Song.* The love of his life. She's moored down at the harbour here.'

Sam's face was giving nothing away. He certainly wasn't about to meet Lia's gaze.

'If she's not secure enough now, it's too late to worry about it. So…no reports of any injuries, then?'

'Not yet.'

Sam's glance swept the room and rested on Hettie. 'Is somebody watching Sefina?'

'Keanu's in there now and then I'm going to take Joni in for a quick visit. She's doing well. In a bit of pain, of course, but she's oriented well enough to use her infusion pump.'

'And Keoni—our cardiac patient?' A frown line appeared on Sam's face as he started a mental run-through of inpatients in the hospital. 'Never mind, I'll go and check myself. I just need some dry clothes.' Finally, he looked directly at Lia. 'I'll get you a pair of scrubs, too, shall I? What size are you?'

There was nothing in the look or his body language that would have given any hint that he might have a very good idea of the size of her body. And its shape and...dear Lord—she could feel a sharp twinge of renewed desire as the thought entered her head—even how it tasted.

It should be a relief that, thanks to Sam's poker face, nobody would guess how well they now knew each other but, oddly, it felt like a putdown. As if that amazing connection they'd found didn't mean anything at all. That it was already forgotten.

'I can do that.' Anahera pushed her chair back. 'Come with me, Lia. I'll get you a towel for your hair, too. You look like you went swimming. Aren't you cold?'

'A bit.' But the goose-bumps she could now see on her arms didn't really have anything to do with her body temperature, did they? They'd been a physical response to the dismissal Sam had just dealt out.

It had been easy to pick up that Jack would have been up for a quick fling with a visitor to this island. Had she somehow missed the signals that Sam was just as likely to make the most of an unexpected opportunity, as well?

'There's a few sizes of overalls in the change room,'

Jack said. 'And some waterproof undergear. You might want to be ready in case you get a callout.'

The radio on the desk behind Jack crackled as if it had been waiting for the right moment. Jack pulled the headphones perched on his head down over his ears and leaned forward to press the button on the microphone.

'Wildfire Rescue Base receiving. Go ahead...'

Voices outside the staffroom made it difficult to hear what was being relayed through the crackling on the radio and Lia found herself edging towards the wall as more people came in. A small girl ran towards Anahera.

'Mumma... It's *windy*...'

Vailea was right behind the child. She was wearing a light rainproof poncho and pushed the hood back from her head.

'Some of the villagers were too frightened to stay at home. I've brought them up here and put them in the waiting room in Outpatients. One of the lads hurt his arm when they were trying to secure the boats earlier. He might need looking at.'

'I'll do that.' Hettie got to her feet. 'Could you keep Joni with Hana?'

'No...' The small girl shook her head. 'I want to stay with Mumma.'

'You can't, sweetheart.' Anahera kissed her daughter's head. 'Mummy's got to work because people need looking after. You be a good girl and stay with Nana.'

'But—'

'I have to go. Look, Lia's all wet. I've got to go and find her some new clothes.'

'I'm wet, too...'

'Not very. You've got your raincoat on.' Anahera stepped back as Hettie passed Joni into Vailea's arms. 'You might want to take a stack of towels into the waiting room. I expect everybody will be fairly wet.'

Vailea was staring at Lia. 'You're completely soaked,' she said. 'What on earth have you been doing?'

But Lia was watching Jack. By the look on his face, he'd heard something serious on the radio transmission that he was about to discuss with Sam. By focusing on the two men, she could filter out the sound of the women around her.

'The trees coming down caused a landslide. Rocks and mud. There's a whole family trapped in one of the houses, by the sound of it. And others that have been injured. They need help.'

'I'll go.' Sam's face was grim. 'We've got to get some medical cover on Atangi anyway. We haven't got anyone at the clinic other than Marnie and even a few minor injuries will be more than she can cope with.'

Lia stepped past Vailea. 'I'll come, too. Show me where to get a kit together.'

'I brought the packs down from the chopper when I knew we wouldn't be flying anywhere. They're in the change room where the overalls are.'

Sam was shaking his head. 'It's dangerous,' he said. 'The only way we can get there is by boat and I can't let anyone else risk that trip.'

Lia met his gaze. 'You're going.'

'I know what I'm doing. And it's my boat.' There was more than the acknowledgment of a grim situation showing on his face now. This was a man who wouldn't hesitate to put himself in danger for others.

The sort of man that people could rely on. Someone honourable and trustworthy.

Someone that deserved respect and Sam had just won a huge amount of hers.

'He does know what he's doing.' Jack nodded. 'Sam's got sea water for blood. I'd go with him. You may not need to use your boat, though, mate. Ky's rounding up some manpower. I'll call him back and see if they can launch the coastguard vessel and come to get you. It's a lot more powerful than your runabout and it'll fit more people. I could come with you.'

'You're needed here. I want someone who knows what they're doing with the radio and can coordinate any rescue missions needed. Give me one of the hand-held sets.'

'And me.' Lia held out her hand. She knew she was scowling at Sam with a 'don't try and stop me' expression. 'This is my job,' she told him. 'You might not have read my CV but I've had training in urban search and rescue. I'm not going to sit around here when I know that there's a family trapped in a collapsed building. There are probably *children* in there...'

'It'll be rough,' Sam warned. But there was something that looked like admiration in his gaze. 'Are you sure you want to come?'

There was something more than admiration in the way he was looking at her.

Something like the feeling she was getting, perhaps? That they might both be very good at the jobs they did but together...they were capable of something even better. Something extraordinary even—like beating the danger of a huge storm and saving lives?

Maybe it wasn't appropriate to smile but Lia couldn't

help it. And Sam might not be smiling back but she could swear there was a gleam in his eyes that suggested he was smiling inside.

His slow nod, however, was completely serious. 'Let's go.'

CHAPTER FIVE

IT WAS ONE thing to expect a bit of excitement in taking on a new adventure but, in her wildest dreams, Lia could not have conjured up this scenario.

At sea—as night fell—in the teeth of a tropical cyclone. Wearing a set of bright orange overalls beneath her life jacket and hanging on to her seat with both hands to stop herself becoming airborne as the boat surged and dropped over the massive swells beyond the coral reefs.

A uniformed islander was at the wheel of the powerful motor boat and Sam was standing beside him. Somehow, they were both keeping their footing as they navigated the angry stretch of ocean between Wildfire Island and the much bigger settlement of Atangi. In calm weather the journey probably only took about fifteen minutes but this seemed to be taking forever and, despite hanging on and bracing herself, Lia was over the pummelling.

Sam turned and mouthed something at her that looked like, 'You okay?'

She loosened the grip of one hand long enough to give him a thumbs-up sign. He nodded and turned back, pointing forward at something as he tilted his head towards the man beside him, shouting something that Lia couldn't catch. Hopefully, he was pointing towards their destination. Landing and getting off the boat wasn't going to be easy but Lia was impatient to get there and get on with the rescue mission.

She had all the medical gear she might need in the heavy pack Jack had provided and Sam had another one he would be carrying on his back. Looking around this well-equipped rescue vessel, Lia took note of coiled ropes, blankets and tools and the Stokes basket rescue stretcher that could be loaded up with the extra supplies. Would there be other people available to help carry it or were the able-bodied men of the villages already at the scene of the landslide, desperately trying to dig out the people who had been buried or trapped?

Thankfully, the sea was a little calmer once they were within the reef protecting Atangi. The driving rain made visibility poor but this side of the island was not taking the full force of the wind and there were people waiting to help secure and offload the boat. There was still enough of a swell to make the task challenging. Lia passed the medical packs to Sam, who threw them up onto the jetty where they were caught by a big man wearing a police officer's uniform.

'Shall we take the Stokes basket? And some ropes and things?'

'Good thinking. Ky?' Sam waved the police officer closer. 'Have we got some manpower to help carry some more supplies?'

'Sure thing. We'll load whatever looks useful into the jeep. I'll have to drive you to the other side. It'll take too long to walk.'

Sam timed the roll of the boat and leapt up onto the

jetty when they had offloaded what they wanted. Then he crouched and held out his hand to Lia.

'Wait until the boat's coming up. Then grab my hand. You'll have to be ready to jump.'

His grip on her hand was tight and the upward tug firm enough to make the leap onto the solid wood of the jetty easy. The pull was almost too firm, in fact, because it pulled Lia right against his body and he had to steady them both by catching her shoulders to stop her forward momentum.

For just the tiniest moment, when their faces were so close together, Sam's gaze met hers and Lia was aware of a surge of…something. Energy maybe. This wasn't sexual but it was just as exciting. They were about to start a task with unknown dimensions and danger involved. And they were doing it together. The shared glance was like a pact had been made. They would be doing whatever needed to be done but they would also be watching each other's back.

Taking care of each other.

There was no time for any significant moments after that. Having piled into the jeep along with all their gear, they were bouncing along a rough road that led out from the main township, going off-road in places to avoid fallen trees. The windscreen wipers were failing to cope with the deluge of water pouring down and the vehicle was rocking in the wind. More than once Ky had to stop the vehicle when they came across people who were fighting their way along the edge of the road.

He would roll down the window and yell, 'Anybody hurt? I've got the doc on board.'

If the answer was no, the islanders were advised to take care and make their way to the school hall. As they got further away from the township, the advice was to get to the nearest dwelling and stay inside, away from any flying debris.

If the answer was yes, Sam and Lia would assess and apply minimal first aid. A dressing to keep a laceration clean until it could be sutured later. A splint on a broken arm. These people were walking wounded and they could wait. Where they were headed there were likely to be injuries serious enough to need urgent medical intervention for people to survive.

The landslide was bigger than any of them had expected. There was no way to take the jeep off the track and drive around it. Huge old trees high up the side of the mountain must have been torn out by their roots, dislodging massive rocks that had kicked off a crescendo of destruction. Several metres high, the tangle of rock, mud, tree trunks and vines would have to be scaled on foot.

And Ky had messages coming through thick and fast on his radio. Roofs were lifting from houses in the township, with sheets of tin coming loose to threaten anybody still outside. The scene in the school hall was chaotic and the chain of command was not clear enough with Ky missing. Relaying instructions wasn't enough and the tone of the broadcasts was getting steadily more urgent.

'I'll have to go back,' Ky told Sam and Lia as he stopped with the headlights of the jeep shining on the mountain of landslide debris. 'I know you'll need help but, as far as we know, there's only a few people affected here. I'm responsible for the whole Atangi community right now.'

'Go,' Sam said. 'We'll find out exactly what we're

dealing with and let you know. Can you send the jeep back when we need transport?'

'I'm going to have to call in any available vehicles to get people to safety. I'll find something to send out here as soon as possible.'

Lia used her shoulder to get her door open against the wind. 'I'll get the packs out. What will we do with the stretcher?'

'We'll leave it here for now.' Sam had his door open too. 'The important thing is to find out what's going on. I'm just hoping the building isn't under this lot or we might find there's nothing we *can* do.'

Ky left the engine running as he helped them offload the gear. About to climb back into the driver's seat, he looked up, shielding his eyes from the rain.

'Hey…' he shouted.

Lia and Sam, hoisting their backpacks into position, turned to look up, as well. A man was clambering over the pile, wearing nothing but shorts and a shredded T-shirt. His feet were bare.

'Come,' he yelled, catching hold of a protruding tree branch as his feet slipped in the mud. 'Quick. My wife…my children…I need help…'

Lia was already moving. 'It's climbable,' she said over her shoulder to Sam. 'He's done it in bare feet and we've got boots.' She flicked on the headlamp attached to her helmet. 'Stay there,' she called up to the islander. 'We're coming. What's your name?'

'Afi.'

'I'm Lia. And this is Sam. Okay, Afi—take us where we need to go.'

Talk about courage.

Sam was behind Lia as she tackled the climb and he

was having a hard job keeping up with her pace. Even with the heavy pack on her back, she was hauling herself up with a speed and grace that were astonishing. It wasn't a stupid headlong rush, though. She was testing branches and rocks as she followed their guide to see if they could still take her weight and choosing an alternative if they couldn't. At one point she hesitated briefly before grasping a thick vine.

'Are there snakes here?'

'Not here. We've got a nasty little adder on Wildfire but it sticks to the marshes around the lagoon.'

Her hand curled around the dark coil that could have been the tail of a snake and she was off again. It didn't take long to get to the top and then she stopped still for longer this time, staring down at whatever she could see in front of her—assessing the scene for dangers and whatever task lay ahead. Sam was by her side seconds later.

'Holy heck...'

The landslide had caught one side of the house, pushing it off any foundations it might have had and twisting it sideways. The tin roof was buckled, half of it buried under rocks with sheets bent and ripped, lethally sharp edges protruding. The wooden framework of the house had collapsed and lay like an oversized child's puzzle of pick-up sticks—flat and tangled. Was there even any space for people to have survived?

'I could hear the baby crying,' Afi said, as he led them down the other side of the obstruction. 'But I can't find her...'

'Were you inside—when it happened?'

'I was in the bedroom trying to fix the shutters. The others were in the back.'

'How many others?'

'My wife, Hika. Our children. Two older ones and the baby.'

And he'd only heard the baby crying? Sam swallowed hard.

'Are there other houses around? Other people who might be hurt?'

'I...I haven't looked.' A sound like a sob broke from the distressed man. 'I... It's my family in there... I had to call for help...'

'We know.' Lia had taken hold of Afi's hands. 'And we're going to do everything we can to help. Are *you* okay? You haven't hurt yourself or been cut by the tin or anything?'

He shook his head. 'I'm not important. I'm fine.'

'You *are* important. Afi, we need you to do something for us.'

'I'll do it.' Afi nodded. 'I want to help. Just tell me...'

'We need to know if there are any other people in trouble. You know where the houses are. You can find out for us. We'll stay here and help your family.'

It was the logical way to try and assess the wider area but it was a big ask to expect Afi to move away from where he knew his own family was trapped. Lia was asking for his trust. Had she won it by gentle persuasion rather than issuing a direct order? By the confidence in her reassurance that she and Sam were able to help his loved ones?

She was still holding Afi's hands and eye contact and, to Sam's amazement, he nodded slowly. Then he turned and began to walk away from his destroyed home into the driving rain and wind.

'Be careful,' Lia called after him. 'Keep yourself safe and come back to us as soon as you can.'

He looked back—not at the house but at Lia. A long look, as if he was using her to gather his own strength. And then he was gone, any glimpse of him curtained by the rain and then trees.

Afi had given Lia his trust and he was prepared to do what she had asked of him no matter how hard it was. Sam's heart twisted with something that felt curiously like pride. He barely knew Lia but he knew that that trust had not been misplaced.

The agreement to begin what could be a heartbreaking search was no more than a shared glance between Sam and Lia. They picked their way carefully around the edge of the house. Loose sheets of iron screeched like wounded animals as they bent and scraped in the wind. A piece of wood—maybe a fragment of a shutter—flew past, hitting Sam's helmet, and he had to peer through the water flowing over his visor. He also had to raise his voice to shout as loudly as he could.

'Can anyone hear me? Where are you?'

'Hello?' Lia was yelling, too. 'Can you hear me? *Hika?*'

It was on the far side of the house that they found an opening into the tangle of wood. A triangle of space with the roof forming one side and a broken beam holding up the rest. Lia dropped to a crouch and Sam was able to peer over her shoulder, adding the light from his helmet to hers.

The gap was a tunnel into what had been a room. And right at the end they could see a small child curled up into a ball.

They could also hear a baby crying.

Sam had to step back as Lia started slipping her arms from the straps of the pack.

'I'm going in.'

'No. Not yet. We don't know if it's safe. This could collapse on top of you. We need to find something to shore it up.'

'There's no time. And we haven't got the manpower or equipment to follow those kinds of protocols.' Free of her pack, Lia lay flat on her stomach and slid farther into the gap. 'Are you awake, sweetheart?' she called. 'Can you look at me?'

The child's face appeared from the ball of small person but one look at the bright light shining in was enough to make it disappear again. If, by some miracle, this little one was unhurt, they were too terrified to co-operate.

'*Kia orana*,' Sam called gently, using the island language. 'What's your name, little one?'

The small face remained hidden.

'What did you say?' Lia asked. 'Do the children here not speak English?'

'Everybody's more or less bilingual. Some prefer to use their own language.'

'So how do I say "hello"?'

'*Kia orana*. But you'll be understood. Don't worry about having to translate things.'

'Okay.' Lia nodded. And then started wriggling forward.

'Come out,' Sam ordered. 'I'll go in.'

'I'm smaller,' Lia said. 'Let me get this one out and see if there's any access farther in.'

There was nothing Sam could do to stop her and she was right. She had more chance of getting into a small space than he did.

And there were children here. He wouldn't have

let anyone stop him if he knew there was a chance of saving them.

Lia was his kind of person.

There was more room to move as Lia got farther beneath the debris. She could see into other pockets of space and the hope that they would find more members of this family alive got stronger. Nobody else was immediately visible so the rules of triaging a multi-casualty scene couldn't be applied. If they had been, she would have had to simply check the first victim she found and then move on to assess the others so that she could then decide on who had the highest priority for treatment. In this case, she was going to have to do the best she could with each step, rather than consider the big picture.

Sam had been right. She was breaking rules and not putting her own—and other rescuers'—safety first but this pile of building wreckage was likely to be highly unstable. Who knew how long they might have to get anyone out who was still alive?

She reached the child and pulled off her gloves so that she could feel the temperature of the skin, which was reassuringly warm. She could see the small chest rising and falling so there was no breathing difficulty so then she ran her hands swiftly over the little body, doing a rapid check for any obvious injuries or bleeding.

'Hey,' she said. 'It's okay, sweetheart. I'm here to look after you. Do you know where Mummy is?'

'Mumma…' The child's head came up and she burst into tears. Small arms moved to wrap themselves around Lia's neck and cling hard. '*Mumma…*'

Lia heard another sound from somewhere to one side. Another child crying, or was it a groan from an adult? She needed to move fast and she couldn't do that with a terrified child in her arms. She wriggled backwards, one hand pressed to a frizzy mop of hair to try and protect the child from any falling debris.

Sam was waiting to take the child.

'I've heard something else,' Lia told him. 'I'm going back in. I think this one's okay. Nothing obvious, anyway.'

She got past where the child had been lying and peered past the fallen beams. She could see a table with broken legs and an overturned couch and...and, yes...the bare foot and lower leg of an adult person who was lying in the space where the back of the couch had caught on the tilted table.

'*Hika*... Can you hear me?'

The response was a groan. And then a voice that she had to strain to hear.

'Help me... Help my babies...'

'I'm coming. Hold on...'

But how could she get as far as the couch? A tilted beam was blocking her way. There was enough space to kneel in front of it but there was no way she could lift the heavy piece of wood out of the way. And if she moved it, would something else collapse?

She needed help.

She needed Sam.

'I'm here.'

Good grief...had she been talking aloud to herself? And why had Sam taken the risk of squeezing himself into that narrow entrance to the debris?

'Where's the little girl?'

'Afi's back. He's brought his neighbours, as well. They're all okay. They want to help.'

'I can see Hika. And I think the baby's with her. I can't get through here. Maybe there's another way in from the other side?'

'Let me try moving that beam. If I can lift it, it looks like that pile is solid enough to support it.'

'If you can just lift it a bit, I could get through.'

Sam was moving closer. His arm was around Lia as he edged sideways to get his shoulder under the beam. His face was only a few inches from hers.

'But then you might get stuck on the other side,' he said.

The concern in his face wrapped itself tightly around Lia's heart. A tiny part of her brain told her that it was simply professional concern but she could feel his arm still around her and her face was close enough to his for the memory of what it was like to kiss him to surface. The mix of thinking about someone genuinely caring and kissing her at the same time made the squeezing sensation in her chest so big it was too hard to take a breath.

A vicious gust of wind lifted the section of roof above the tunnel of debris and it came down again with a sickening crunch and a cloud of dust. The whole, unstable structure around them seemed to shift and then settle.

There was more than concern in Sam's face now. If she gave him the smallest opportunity, he would order her out of this space to keep her safe. And maybe she would go. Imagine what her family would think if they knew she was putting herself in danger like this? What it would be like for them if she didn't make it out herself?

But if she abandoned this rescue mission, she was

quite sure that Sam would not follow her example. He would stay in here himself and do whatever he could.

And that concern went both ways.

'You've got manpower outside,' Lia said. '*If* I get stuck, you can see what you can move and create another access. It sounds like Hika's injured and it might be impossible to get the Stokes basket in this way. The sooner we do this, the sooner we can all get out.'

For a moment longer, with the wind howling above them and the wreckage creaking ominously around them, Sam held her gaze.

And then one side of his mouth curled upwards into a crooked smile.

'You're quite something, aren't you?'

Lia smiled back at him. 'So are you,' she said. 'Now, get on with it. Show me how strong you are.'

He was strong enough to lift the beam. Not far enough to secure it on a higher level but far enough for Lia to crawl underneath. And there was much more space on the other side. She could actually stand up if she kept her back hunched. She climbed over broken pieces of furniture, her boots crunching on shattered crockery, to get around the table to the gap behind the couch.

A tiny baby was in Hika's arms. A boy who looked about five years old was crouched by his mother's head, holding one of her hands.

'I'm Lia,' she said. 'I've come to get you out.'

'Take my babies first,' Hika said. 'Please… Where's Ema?'

'Your little girl? She's fine. She's outside and being looked after.' Lia was scanning what she could see of the boy and trying to check the baby at the same time. Hika was conscious and talking to her, which was great. It meant that she was breathing well enough for the moment. Even a sideways glance showed Lia that the leg she had spotted earlier was lying at a sickeningly unnatural angle but the priority had to be to get the children to safety.

'What's your name?' she asked the boy.

His face crumpled and he clung closer to his mother.

'He's Rua,' Hika said. And then she groaned again. 'Oh.... It hurts...'

Rua cried more loudly and the baby joined in.

Sam's call could barely be heard over the noise. 'What's happening?'

Lia took the baby from Hika's arms. 'Come with me, Rua. Sam's waiting to help you get outside.'

'No-o...'

'You do as you're told,' Hika growled. With a sob, she prised her son's arms away from her body and pushed him towards Lia. 'Take him...' And then her breath caught in a gasp of pain. Her eyes fluttered shut and her head dropped back.

'Hika?'

She was still breathing but the lack of response told Lia that her level of consciousness had dropped alarmingly. She couldn't do anything with a baby in her arms. Securing the infant against her body, she caught the boy's arm with her free hand and pulled him along beside her.

He resisted enough to make the short journey around the table a struggle. Persuading him to go through the small gap under the beam was even harder. Sam reached through to catch hold of him.

'Your daddy's waiting for you outside,' he told him. 'And your little sister. What's her name?'

'Ema,' Lia supplied.

Rua shook his head. 'I want to stay with Mumma,' he wailed.

'Lia's going to stay with Mumma,' Sam said. 'And she's going to take care of her. You have to come with me, buddy.' He pulled the little boy through the gap and lifted him so that he was on his other side and couldn't get back.

Lia crouched to pass the baby through the gap to Sam. 'This one looks like she's only a few weeks old.'

Sam took the tiny bundle. He ripped the top fastenings of his overalls open and tucked the baby against his body. Then he did up the fastenings so that only the top of the baby's head was visible. For a second, he laid his hand over the fuzz of soft baby hair and then he looked up at Lia.

'I'll get them out,' he said. 'And get the men moving things, but I'll be back as soon as I can. How's Hika?'

'Obvious leg fracture,' Lia told him. 'And her GCS has just dropped. Bring the pack back in with you if you can.'

Moving back to her patient, Lia found herself caught by that unexpected gesture of Sam cradling the baby's head in his hand. Such a gentle, reassuring touch that had probably been so automatic he hadn't realised he was doing it, but it was something she would never forget. A tiny moment in a terrifying ordeal but it gave her something so heartwarming it made her forget her own fear.

And then she was back beside Hika and able to examine her properly, and there was no time to allow herself to think of anything but keeping her patient alive and getting her out to safety.

By the time Sam got back to the other side of the beam with the kit, Lia could hear the sound of shouting from nearby, outside the house.

'The children all seem fine,' he told her. 'Barely a scratch on them.'

'Hika's got an open, mid-shaft femoral fracture,' Lia reported back. 'Limb baselines aren't good. She's got no sensation in her foot and it's cold. And she's lost a lot of blood. I need fluids and pain relief. And a traction splint.'

'I've sent someone back to get the Stokes basket. There's a lot of people out there now. They've come from all over the village. I've been in radio contact with Ky. He's sending out a vehicle to get them into the township. And a chainsaw in case that can help us get better access in here.' The pack was too big to squeeze through the gap so he was opening it as he spoke and passing things through to Lia. A roll of IV gear. Bags of saline and giving sets. The drug roll.

'I need to get in to help you. I'll get someone else to come and lift this beam so I can get underneath.'

Lia shook her head. 'It's too risky. If the roof shifts any further we'll need more than a chainsaw to get us out. I can do everything I need to do medically in here. Hika's going to need surgery when we get her back to the hospital.' She tried to summon a grin for Sam. 'You can take over then, okay?'

He shook his head. 'Bossy, aren't you?'

'You have to be when you grow up with eight siblings.'

'Eight...' Sam's eyes widened. 'I can see I'm not

going to win this argument. Closest I've come to a family is looking after a borrowed dog.'

Not entirely true.

Getting back out of the tunnel took long enough for an old pain to resurface. The amazement of knowing that he was going to become a father and would have more of a family than he'd known since he'd lost both his parents when he'd been barely more than a teenager.

The agony of being told that the baby wasn't his. And that his wife was leaving him to make a new life with the real father of her baby.

And, yes, she would be taking half his fortune with her to ensure that her new life would be the one she'd wanted all along…

It felt appropriate somehow to emerge into a wild storm and get lashed by the wind and rain. His whole life had felt this chaotic back then. So unbearable he'd run away. Taken time out to sail his beloved yacht around the world. Washed up, quite by chance, onto these islands and discovered a new purpose to his life.

And here he was, in a position to help a member of this island community that he'd grown to love so deeply. With a small crowd of islanders looking to him right now, in this storm, to provide the leadership they needed. Enough strong men that they could probably lift a roof if that was what it was going to take to get Hika and Lia out of there safely.

And, dammit, he was going to make that happen. He wasn't about to let Lia's amazing courage end in tragedy. Imagine having to face up to her whole family and tell them he'd been responsible for the world losing such an extraordinary young woman?

It took hours. Long hours of hard physical labour under appalling conditions. They had to be so careful trying to shift building materials when, at any moment, the wind could catch something with lethally sharp edges or protruding nails that could injure or even kill someone. Every so often, Sam would stop the men working completely so he could crawl back through the tunnel and check that Lia was still safe. That Hika was still alive.

'Her blood pressure has come up a little. I'm running another litre of saline. I've got the traction splint on so I'm hoping that will help control the bleeding.'

'You're doing a great job. Are *you* okay?'

'I'm fine. I'd love to get out of here, though…'

'We're getting closer. I'll be with you before you know it.'

'I'm counting on that, Sam.'

She had to keep counting for a while longer but a space was finally cleared and the framework of the roof safe enough on one corner for a group of men to position themselves to lift it. Sam was ready, with Afi by his side and the rigid basket stretcher held between them. The men would have to hold the roof up long enough to get in, get Hika into the stretcher and for them all to get out again. Whether or not they could do it was dependent, in large part, on luck. On a window of time where there was a space between those vicious wind gusts that would make it impossible to control what was left of the iron-clad roof.

Maybe it was luck. Or maybe the ferocity of this

storm was finally beginning to ebb a little as the second day of the cyclone dawned. It didn't matter. Hika was safely secured in the stretcher and there were any number of willing hands to carry her over the landslide to where Ky's jeep was waiting to transfer her. An ancient truck with a flat back had other villagers piling on to be taken to the safety of the school hall.

'Did you check the children again?' Lia looked through the back window of the jeep to where Afi was riding in the cab of the truck, his baby in his arms and his two small children glued to his sides.

'Yes. But I'll get whoever's in the clinic here to keep an eye on them.'

'Can't we take them with us? Hika's going to need her family.'

'There might be other patients who need to come over on the boat.'

'But if there's room?'

There was a plea in Lia's eyes and Sam remembered the hard time he'd given her for using her phone so much on her first day here. Her brother had been undergoing surgery and she'd needed to know what was happening.

She knew more than he did about family. How important it was for them to be together in frightening times.

And she had risked her life for this family. She deserved a medal. She certainly deserved to have a request respected.

Besides, Sam wanted to do this for her. He wanted to see her smile.

'Sure. If there's room, we'll take them all. We'll keep the family together.'

The bump in the road made their drowsy patient groan and Lia's attention was instantly drawn away from Sam.

But she *was* smiling and Sam could feel the glow of it right down to his toes.

CHAPTER SIX

WILDFIRE HOSPITAL—and every member of its staff—were pushed to their limits and beyond that day.

Sam was in Theatre repairing Hika's leg, with another doctor, Keanu, and Hettie and Anahera to assist, so they missed the drama when one wing of the hospital became damaged enough by the wind and rain to mean that patients had to be evacuated to new rooms. Taking Hika to their recovery/intensive care area was the first sign that their working conditions were already stretched. There wasn't enough space for another bed amongst the monitoring equipment.

'We need to keep Keoni in here for continuous cardiac monitoring. Sefina can be moved, though. She's stable.'

'We've lost a lot of beds,' Caroline told them. 'The windows blew in on the north wing. Nobody's had time to clean up the glass and there's a lot of water damage. The power's out on that side, too. Jack's checking the generators but we need to be prepared for some more outages.'

'Can we use some of the consulting rooms in Outpatients?'

'The waiting rooms are overflowing. We've had

more injuries come over from Atangi. It's crazy in there. If it wasn't for that new paramedic, we would have no chance of coping.'

'I'll head there now.'

'I'll come with you,' Hettie said. 'I need to find out where Joni is. Sefina's been asking about him.'

Happy to leave Hika in capable hands, Sam headed for the outpatient area. It wasn't just that it was obviously where extra medical help was needed, he wanted to see Lia again. To tell her that Hika's surgery had gone well.

Maybe to also tell her that it was okay for her to take a break and get some sleep. They had enough people to cope now unless someone else needed emergency surgery. Lia had to be exhausted after the dramatic rescue mission during the night and yet she'd carried on working while he had been tied up in Theatre.

He was exhausted himself.

Not that he was about to go home to rest. There were too many people here, waiting patiently to be seen and treated. It quickly became apparent that it wouldn't be easy to find time to talk to Lia and update her on how her rescued patient was faring. It wasn't only the waiting rooms that were overflowing. Every treatment area was being used. There were lacerations that needed stitching, fractures that needed to be X-rayed and plastered. Bumps and bruises to be assessed and frightened children that needed careful checking to make sure nothing serious was missed.

An hour passed and then another as Sam moved from one patient to the next, weaving his way through the crowded rooms, having to stop and reassure people as he moved past them to the ones who needed attention first. And every time he was on the move, he noticed Lia.

At one point she was crouched in front of a child, splinting a wrist that would probably join the queue for an X-ray. He saw her smiling. Reaching up to stroke a small cheek in a reassuring gesture.

The next time she had her stethoscope against the chest of an old man, a frown on her face as she focused on what she needed to hear instead of the background noise of the crowded room. The smile had been there again, though, before he'd looked away and she'd got one in return from her patient.

Who wouldn't smile back at Lia?

She was carrying a baby when he finally got close enough to speak to her.

'Is that Hika's baby?'

'Yes. She needs a clean nappy. And some food. I'm trying to find Vailea to see if she can help.'

Lia was wearing scrubs now. Baggy pants that completely disguised those long, lean legs. A shapeless top that left her arms bare. Maybe it was the sight of that smooth olive skin that reminded Sam's body of what it knew about this woman. What it felt like to be in very close contact with that skin. It was a moment of intensity that was completely inappropriate right then so he focused on the baby.

'Has she been properly assessed?'

'Only by me. Do you want to see her yourself?'

'Are you happy with her?'

'Yes. I think Hika had her in her arms the whole time. She was well protected.'

This might be only the second day they had worked together but it had been a trial by fire and Sam was more than confident that Lia's assessment would have been as good as his own. 'If you're happy, I'm happy.'

'I've checked all the children. Ema had a few grazes that needed cleaning but that was all. How's Hika?'

'Doing well. The fracture's set and I've started her on IV antibiotics. We've got her blood pressure back up. She's out of danger.'

'Oh...that's fantastic.' Lia's face lit up with satisfaction. 'And what about the blood vessel and nerve damage? I was worried about how bad that was.'

'Her limb baselines were looking good. We'll have to wait until she's properly awake to check sensation and movement and it'll be a while before she's walking again, but I'm confident she'll make a full recovery.'

Lia's smile widened. 'We did good, didn't we?'

Sam smiled back, amused by the childish grammar. 'We did.'

The baby in Lia's arms whimpered and she moved on with her mission of care. Sam stood still for a moment, watching her.

He'd saved lives before. Been out on rescue missions that could have ended in disaster but hadn't. He'd performed surgeries that would prevent a serious injury from becoming a permanent disability more times than he could have counted.

Why did this case feel so special?

Because he'd been working with Lia?

Because he was increasingly blown away by how amazing she was? She was not only highly skilled in the assessment and treatment of patients, she had the ability to connect with them on a personal level. She cared about them.

She had not only demonstrated an impressive level

of courage, she was now showing that she had stamina to match.

Lia Roselli was one of a kind—that was for sure. Thank goodness she hadn't been injured herself last night. As Sam took yet another patient from the waiting room for treatment, he remembered how it had felt when he'd known he was allowing her to stay in danger in that house. When the roof had shifted in the wind and reminded them both of just how dangerous the situation was.

Her safety had seemed more important than anything else. Like it had when he'd been holding her in his arms in his bed and they'd heard the sound of breaking glass and he'd promised that he would keep her safe.

He'd shocked himself then. The danger signs of falling for someone had been flashing brightly enough to make him back away so fast he hadn't even taken the time to analyse and label the emotion.

Was it even harder now? Now that he knew how brave and tough she was? And what a kind heart she had?

No. Okay, he'd broken his rule about hooking up with an attractive newcomer. And yes, he was more than impressed with her personality as well as her body, but anything more than that was simply the aftermath of having shared an adrenaline-fuelled experience. And exhaustion.

This was a fling—that was all. One that would probably be more memorable than any holiday hook-ups he'd ever had before, but that was all it was. All it ever could be.

He just wasn't thinking straight, and that was hardly

surprising. A few hours' sleep would fix that and that would happen.

Eventually.

He was unstoppable, wasn't he?

Lia's legs were beginning to feel like jelly and the occasional wave of dizziness told her that if she didn't catch some sleep soon, she wouldn't be safe to be working with patients.

But Sam wasn't even slowing down and he'd been on his feet just as long as she'd been. He'd had the additional stress of the long surgery on Hika, as well, and now he was not only taking on the management of the cases that were beyond her own scope of practice, he was going back into the waiting room again and again, as the numbers of people waiting gradually lessened.

She had spotted him almost every time she'd gone to find a new patient, or taken someone to the X-ray department or through to the area where Hettie was being kept busy, applying plaster casts to the surprising number of Colles' fractures where both children and elderly had fallen onto an outstretched hand.

She'd seen how long it took for Sam to move through the groups of islanders because of the number of people who wanted to be the ones he chose to treat. He was given the respect of a true leader—royalty, almost—and yet he was clearly part of the community. He was approachable enough that everyone knew they would get the reassurance they needed.

He was their doctor and they trusted him. More than that, he'd been here long enough to have earned more than simply respect and trust. More than once Lia saw him offer a touch of reassurance to an adult or pick up a child who happily wrapped their arms around his neck. And she'd seen the expression on the faces of the mothers and the people who had been given words of encouragement or the squeeze of a hand. It was impossible not to get the impression that Sam was loved by these people.

Had she really thought that he didn't fit here? That it looked like he was playing a role in a movie? There could be no doubt that he belonged here. That he was one of these people, despite standing out as looking so very different with his much paler skin and the sun-bleached blondness of his hair.

What had brought him here? Lia wondered. And why had he stayed long enough to become such an integral part of this isolated community?

Maybe it was the level of utter weariness she was trying to push through as she kept going that made it difficult to shut out thoughts that were even less appropriate than noticing Sam's status as a doctor here. Dislocated thoughts that were more snatches of emotion than conscious recall of sequences of events. They didn't interfere with the job she was doing, but they slipped into the back of her mind every time she noticed him.

Like the memory of that first kiss—down on the beach, when the storm had first broken. That moment when something amazing had made it so much more than any kiss she had ever experienced.

That firm grip of his hand around hers as he'd led her up the track to his house.

Making love…

As Lia went back into the waiting room yet again, she stopped for a moment. There were fewer people here now and it didn't look as if any of them were seriously injured. There were no bloodstained, makeshift bandages on limbs. Nobody holding an arm as if they were scared to allow it any movement. No crying children being carried in the arms of a parent. There was no sign of Sam, for once, either.

She really did feel dizzy now. How long had it been since she'd eaten something? Or had a drink of water even?

'Are you okay?'

No wonder she hadn't spotted Sam. He'd been behind her.

'A bit woozy. I'm thinking I might need to find something to eat.'

'Come with me. I've been told that Vailea's left a mountain of sandwiches in the staffroom for us.'

'But…' Wearily, Lia turned her head to scan the waiting room.

'The urgent cases have all been seen. Keanu and Ana have had a break and they're going to take over. We've been ordered to stand down for a few hours. You won't need to come back on duty until tomorrow morning, unless things get crazy again.'

It was a relief to follow Sam. To sit down for a little while and eat the most delicious egg salad sandwiches Lia had ever tasted and to wash them down with more than one cup of wonderfully strong, sweet tea.

'Are you going to go home to sleep?'

'I'll have to. There isn't a spare bed anywhere here.'

'Is it my imagination or has the wind died down?'

Sam smiled. 'The worst is over. People are starting to go home. They want to check on their properties and neighbours. We may get a few more patients from the outer islands but it sounds like Atangi got the worst of the storm and I think we've dealt with almost all of it. And nobody's died, as far as we know. Thanks to you,' he added. 'Hika was the most seriously injured and if you hadn't been with her, she might not have made it. She lost a lot of blood from that fracture.'

Lia could feel her eyes drifting shut. Not even Sam's praise could make her smile this time.

'Come on. I'll walk you home. I have to go past your quarters to get to mine.'

The wind was definitely less ferocious as they walked out of the hospital grounds. It was easy to walk unaided, which meant there was no need for Sam to offer a hand.

There was no need for him to stop when they reached Lia's hut, either, but he did. He rubbed his forehead as though he was too tired to remember something he had intended to say and then he looked up and met her gaze.

She could see how exhausted he was. She could also see something that looked like confusion. As though he had something he wanted to ask but, at the same time, he was talking himself out of asking.

Was he thinking about asking her to go back to his quarters?

To sleep with him?

That would be all they were capable of doing but Lia would have said yes in a heartbeat.

She wanted to be with him. Just to sleep. Together. To be close.

And that was the moment she knew she was lost. She was falling in love with this man. Maybe it had already happened and she hadn't noticed. It might have been the way he'd looked at her when he'd known he was putting her in danger by leaving her under the wreckage of Hika's house.

Or it might have been the way she'd felt after she'd seen him tuck that tiny baby against his chest and cradle its head in his hand.

The realisation was enough of a shock to make Lia catch her breath. Had it shown in her face? Was that why Sam broke the eye contact and actually stepped back to put more space between them?

'Sleep well, Lia. I'll see you back at the hospital tomorrow morning.'

She couldn't find any words. And if she opened her mouth, who knew what words might escape? Something crazy like, 'I love you'?

She'd known him for how long? Just a couple of days. Long days, certainly, under conditions that made you get to know someone very quickly, but still…

It was ridiculous.

Much safer to nod and turn away herself.

To use the last of her energy to reconnect with her real life. She'd been able to send a single text message to her family early in the day to tell them she was safe and not to worry about any news they might hear about the weather conditions around these islands, but there had been more than a dozen messages in return and she had to check them all in case there was something she needed to know about Nico's recovery or test results. Or that something had happened to Angel. Her beloved niece had had far more than her share of physical problems and unexpected hospital admissions in her short life so far.

But all was well back home and the messages were

all about her family's concern for her wellbeing. They all missed her and wanted her safely back home, and the love that came through was enough to bring a lump to Lia's throat and more than a few tears that she was too tired to even wipe away. She sent the same message to everybody. She was safe. The worst of the cyclone was over. She'd be home before long and she couldn't wait to see them all.

It was true. No matter how exciting her time here was already proving to be, or how she might think she felt about Sam Taylor, she had her real life to go back to and she wouldn't trade that for anything.

The shower felt wonderful when she finally gave her battered-feeling body the luxury of standing beneath the rain of hot water, but it didn't wash away the feeling that her life might have just changed forever.

The softness of her bed was equally appreciated but, even as sleep rushed up to claim her, Lia couldn't shake the impression that something had gone wrong here.

Finding someone had been the last thing on her mind when she'd come to Wildfire. She wasn't looking. She wasn't interested. At this particular time in her life she couldn't afford—or didn't want—the complications that came with falling in love.

But there it was. She'd been ambushed. Hadn't had enough warning to put up any defences and now it was too late.

Or maybe not. She was too tired to think straight. Maybe things would look different when she woke up.

Things did look different.

Clearer.

It wasn't just that the rain had stopped and the cloud

cover had thinned enough to make the daylight feel normal. Or that the hospital was far less crowded and it felt like things were well under control.

The moment Lia walked into the staffroom and saw Sam, it felt like she had taken off a pair of emotional sunglasses that had been clouding her vision.

He looked…gorgeous.

Well, actually, he looked a bit rugged. His hair was tousled and spiky. There were deep lines around his eyes and he obviously hadn't shaved in quite some time because she knew how rough it would feel if she stroked her fingers along the line of his jaw.

And that was when she knew that the difference sleep had made was to make things worse. Because all she wanted to do was exactly that—to stroke his jaw and touch those lines of weariness. To make sure he'd had something to eat and then tuck him up into a soft bed and let him sleep.

The urge to look after him was as strong as it would have been if she was looking at Nico. Or Angel. Or any of the people who were the most important in her life.

And mixed into that desire to care for him was an underlying desire of a very different kind. Something that her family could never give her.

Something that had been missing from her life for a very long time.

On top of that, there was a sinking feeling that this was a personal disaster. She belonged in a very different world from Sam and in a matter of days she would be returning to that world and leaving him behind, and she knew that was going to hurt.

How weird that you could know so much in the

space of a glance and that nobody else would even notice.

Sam hadn't even looked up from the mug of coffee he was holding in his hand. Jack was sitting at the radio desk, headphones on, fiddling with a waveband control, and Hettie was watching something turning inside the microwave oven. No. Her eyes were closed. Maybe she had fallen asleep on her feet.

'Hi.' Lia pulled out a chair to sit down at the table. 'I'm getting the feeling I'm the only one who's been sleeping.' She risked only a brief glance at Sam as he looked up. 'How many hours did you get?'

'A few. We had a woman in labour brought over from Atangi and she was in trouble with a footling presentation. Ended up needing a Caesarean.'

'I'm going home right now,' Hettie said. 'As soon as I've heated this wheat bag for one of my patients. I think I'm going to sleep until tomorrow.'

'I'm good,' Jack said. 'I've been sleeping on and off in here between radio calls.'

'Have there been many?'

'Not since last night. I got a bit of one a while back, though, and it got cut off. I'm trying some other bands in case it's someone who's not using our frequency.' He turned the dial again, tilting his head to one side as he listened.

Hettie left the room and Lia could feel Sam looking at her but she kept her gaze on Jack. She didn't want him to guess what was going on in her head right now. Or her heart, for that matter. Especially her heart. He couldn't possibly feel the same way. Becoming aware of just the possibility of being in love with him must have sent out a vibe that had made him step away from her.

She was a visitor in his life. Like many others must had been. The last thing he'd want would be a complication that made it a nuisance. Something too heavy to be fun.

And even if she was only going to be here for a short time, she didn't want to throw away the chance to be alone with him again. To be close.

Or maybe that was the most sensible thing she could do. The closer she allowed herself to get, the harder it was going to be to walk away.

Her head started spinning and she closed her eyes, only to open them smartly as she heard the sharp crackle of the radio transmission Jack had picked up.

'Mayday...Mayday... This is the yacht *Eclipse*. Mayday...Mayday... Is anyone receiving?'

Jack pressed the transmission button on the microphone. 'Wildfire Rescue Base receiving you loud and clear. What is your location? Over...'

Adrenaline coursed through Lia and her gaze flew to meet Sam's. Any impression of exhaustion had vanished. He might still look totally dishevelled but he was as focused as Lia was.

Ready for anything.

They both were.

Minutes later, Jack was still sitting at the desk as the transmission ended, flanked by Sam and Lia on either side as he pointed at a spot on a map.

'He's here. If he's drifting, he's going to end on this reef.'

'He can't do anything but drift. He's lost his mast and he's broken his arm so badly he can't get his engine started.' Sam was frowning. 'The wind might have dropped but the swells will still be massive. He hasn't got a chance.'

'Send out the coastguard launch?' Jack was watching a computer screen now, as he brought up a comprehensive weather forecast.

'It might take too long. And the pilot's been stood down for a break, hasn't he? He's been up all night.'

'Wind's fine for flying. Might be a bit choppy but it's safe enough.'

'That would make it a winch job.' Lia took a deep breath. 'I'm up for it but we'd have to have a third crew member to operate the winch. Is anybody available that's qualified?'

There was a moment's silence.

Jack turned his head to glance up at Sam, who nodded his head slowly.

'Yes. I am.'

CHAPTER SEVEN

SAM WAS ON top of this.

If he'd been in any real danger of falling for Lia, he wouldn't be the least bit happy about sitting in the back of this helicopter with her, knowing that she was about to risk her life again for the sake of saving someone else's.

This was her job and she knew what she was doing.

Sam knew what he was doing, too. He could operate a winch as well as anybody and he'd done sea rescues like this before, both as the winch operator and the medic who was being lowered on board a vessel to bring a patient up. He knew the dangers. How you had to avoid the winch line getting caught on any of the masts or wires above deck level. That the moment of contact that would come with getting on board had to be meticulously timed with the swell of the sea so the deck didn't rush up and break your legs.

He could do that for Lia. He could keep her safe so that she could do her job. They'd get her on board and she could do whatever had to be done to treat this lone sailor who'd been caught in the storm and get him safely harnessed and attached to her own body. Then they'd pull them both up and be back at the hospital within the hour. The yacht would have to be sacrificed but that was one of the risks of the sailing game. Boats could be replaced. Lives couldn't.

So he was happy about doing this job and that meant that he had Lia safely tucked into the category of a colleague, and that was more of a relief than he cared to admit. It didn't mean he didn't care about her. Of course it didn't. He cared just as much as he had when she'd been in danger under that house but he also knew how capable she was. How much she cared about her family and how important it was for her to get home in one piece. She knew what she was doing and she wouldn't be taking any stupid risks.

Jack had been right about how rough some of these air pockets still were. And he'd been right about the size of the swells they could see beneath them. A good ten metres, he estimated, and the tops were breaking in rolls of foam that made it hard to spot their target.

'There it is. Three o'clock.'

'Roger… Copy that.' The helicopter tipped as Jack began circling. 'Turning downwind.'

Lia was checking her harness and moving so that she would be ready for permission to move onto the skid of the helicopter when the door was opened.

'Secure aft.' Sam focused on the job at hand. 'Checking winch power.'

The helicopter rocked but Jack seemed happy enough with his control. 'Speed back. Clear door.'

'Door back and locked,' Sam responded. 'Bringing hook inboard.'

He handed the hook to Lia who attached it to her harness, checking the pit pin was secure and nodding at Sam to show she was happy.

'Moving Lia to door. Clear skids.'

'Clear skids.' Jack was happy for Lia to move out and stand on the skids.

'Clear to boom out,' Sam said a few seconds later.

'Clear,' Jack responded.

Lia grinned at Sam in the moment before she stepped off the skid.

'Don't drop me, okay?'

He grinned back. 'No worries.'

She was spinning a bit as he lowered her but she put her arms out to slow the movement and her voice was calm in his headphones.

'Ten metres…eight… Hold for a bit. There's a big swell coming. Let's aim for the top of the next one.'

Jack was doing a brilliant job keeping the helicopter hovering as steadily as the conditions allowed. He was looking down at Lia. If anything went wrong, his responsibility was to keep his aircraft and those on board safe. There was a button on the dashboard that could fire an explosion that would cut the winch cable if it got tangled on anything and prevent them being brought down. Sam had access to the other explosive device. He'd never had to even think about using it, though, and he didn't expect to this time.

How it happened was hard to say. Maybe the yacht tipped unexpectedly as it reached the top of the swell. Perhaps it was the air pocket that jolted the helicopter. Or maybe it was a gust of wind that made the broken end of the mast swing on the wires that were still attached.

Whatever it was, it happened in a split second.

The cry from Lia was wordless but it was all too obvious the winch cable had caught.

'Cut the cable,' Jack yelled, as he wrestled with the controls of the helicopter.

And Sam had to do it. A moment's hesitation and it could all be over for all of them. The helicopter would drop like a stone, probably right on top of the yacht. At least this way Lia had a chance. She was within a few feet of the deck and she wouldn't land in the ocean.

Sam pressed the button before he could give himself any time to think any further. The helicopter swooped upwards but he was looking down, leaning out of the open door.

He saw Lia fall with a sickening thump. Saw her roll across the deck and for a heart-stopping moment he thought she would simply slide off and into the sea, but something stopped her.

'Lia?' Jack was on the radio. 'Talk to us. Are you okay?'

They could see her lying there. Then they saw someone emerge from below the deck. The yachtsman they had been coming to rescue was moving slowly, his arms crossed as he tried to protect the broken limb that was making it impossible for him to control his vessel. He reached Lia and knelt down beside her. Then he looked up at the helicopter and seemed to be nodding his head.

Did that mean she was alive? Conscious?

'Lia...' Sam shouldn't have to shout. His voice should be coming through loud and clear on the inbuilt headphones in Lia's helmet. Her voice should be just as clear through her microphone but there was no sound to be heard other than an ominous buzzing.

'Radio might be out,' Jack said grimly. 'She could have hit her helmet hard on landing and damaged it.'

'She's not moving.'

'There's nothing we can do.' Jack was turning them away. 'We'll have to send a boat out. There's still time before they get too close to the reef.'

'Wait… I want to see if she's moving.'

But Jack kept going and that was the right thing to do. They had to get the coastguard to launch and get out here as fast as possible. Whether Lia was conscious or not made no difference.

Except that it felt like Sam's heart was being ripped out with every passing second that was taking them farther away.

Just colleagues?

Hardly.

A bit of a fling?

Just as much of a lie.

Right now, Lia's life felt more important than his own. Sam had never felt like this about anybody in his entire life.

Because he'd never been so absolutely in love with someone before?

'Take me to Atangi,' he told Jack. 'If anyone's taking the launch out, it's going to be me.'

Lia wasn't injured.

The bump had been hard enough for it to take a short time to figure that out, though, and she'd instinctively stayed motionless until she could identify and assess any parts of her body that might be hurting in case it was important not to move. If she'd broken her neck, for example.

She'd certainly hit her head hard enough to break her radio. She could hear the men above her, albeit through a heavy crackling, and she responded to Jack to tell him she thought she was okay but her transmission obviously hadn't got back to them.

And then she'd heard Sam shout her name and she recognised the note of desperation in the call because that was exactly what she would feel like if she thought something terrible had happened to *him*.

Did that mean that the feelings she had for Sam were not as one-sided as she'd assumed?

The thought was almost as stunning as the blow to her body had been. She tried to move. All she needed to do was to get to her feet and give them a wave but nothing was co-operating fast enough and now she had a man kneeling beside her and demanding her attention, asking if she was all right.

Lia wiggled her feet inside her boots and clenched and unclenched her fists. That felt normal. She took a deep breath without difficulty and let it out, noting with relief the absence of any pain. That fall could have easily broken a rib or two, which would have made it very difficult to move around on a rocking boat.

The crackling and buzzing in her helmet grew louder and she could only catch a word here and there as Jack and Sam talked to each other. She heard mention of a boat and something about the time before they would hit the reef, but she couldn't tell if it had been a hopeful statement or a prediction of doom.

Fear kicked in and gave her the strength to move properly. The man beside her was cradling what looked like a badly broken arm. If anyone was going to be able to start an engine and then steer this yacht and keep it out of danger for as long as it took to get a sea rescue under way, it would have to be her.

Her legs were working. And her arms. Lia pulled them into action and got to her knees and then her feet. She had to cling to the solid object that had stopped that horrible slide across the deck for a second or two until a wave of dizziness passed, but then she took another deep breath and looked up—just in time to see the dot that was the helicopter disappearing into the distance.

Sam...

It felt like an anguished shout inside her head but it came out as no more than a whisper.

Would she even see him again, let alone feel his arms around her?

She had to do whatever it took to make that happen. Lia turned to the stranger beside her.

'I'm Lia,' she told him. 'Show me how to get this boat under control and then we'll do something about that arm of yours.'

The pilot of the islands' coastguard vessel had been dragged from his much-needed sleep. He made sure the boat got launched swiftly but, adding up the flight time getting to the harbour and finally heading out to sea, nearly an hour had passed since they'd abandoned the yacht and its occupants. They were in such trouble, and who knew whether they were still afloat or if the worst had happened and they'd smashed against that reef?

The pilot was as determined as Sam to get to where they needed to be in the shortest possible time. The double engines of the powerful boat were roaring at full tilt. They cut through the rise of the swells, becoming airborne as often as not before landing with a bang and crescendo of engine noise to tackle the next swell.

Jack had come with them. They might need all the

hands they could get to transfer people from one vessel to another in conditions like this, and he wasn't about to let anyone else take up the space for crew.

'You're not leaving me behind,' he'd said. 'That's Lia out there and I'm responsible for the safety of my chopper crew.'

And that was it, in a nutshell. Lia was out there and they had no idea if she was even alive. Would they have sent out a boat and push the limits of its capability like this if they'd been going to an unknown victim alone on his yacht?

Yes. But it wouldn't have felt quite this urgent.

As if what they were going to find had the potential to change Sam's life forever.

They got to where they needed to be a lot sooner than any of them had expected.

'They're under power,' the pilot shouted. 'Well away from the reef now.'

How on earth had they managed that?

'I thought the guy on board was too badly injured to start his engines,' Sam said.

'Guess he had some help.' Jack was grinning. 'Strangely, I'm not surprised. Lia's a force to be reckoned with.'

It was more than relief that was trying to overwhelm Sam. He didn't want to allow hope to take over, only to be crushed, but—if that *was* the case, how proud would he be of Lia?

The pilot was on his radio, changing frequencies.

'M'Langi Coastguard to *Eclipse*. Do you read? Over…'

On his third attempt a response came through.

'*Eclipse* receiving. Hey… Thanks for coming. We're glad to see you guys. Over…'

It was a female voice.

Lia's voice.

Sam grabbed the microphone from the pilot.

'*Lia…*are you okay?'

The sound of laughter came through the speakers. 'I'm fine. No thanks to you, mate. You *dropped* me.'

'I'll make it up to you,' Sam promised. He needed to ask about the condition of the yachtsman and they had to find out about the condition the boat was in and whether they needed to evacuate both Lia and the man they'd initially set out to rescue, but the words caught in his throat.

Lia was making a *joke* of this? He wanted to shake her. No. He wanted to take her into his arms and hold on so tightly she could never get away and get herself into danger again.

'I broke the radio…' Lia sounded more serious now. 'Tell Jack I'm sorry.'

'I'm here.' Jack had taken the microphone from Sam. 'No worries. They're still making radios. Fill us in, Lia. What's happening? Are you really okay? How's your patient?'

The questions that Sam should have been asking instead of promising that he would make up for dropping her. Instead of being so stunned by an emotional reaction to hearing her making light of how bad the situation had been that he still had a lump the size of Africa blocking any ability to speak.

'I'm really okay. Got a bit of a bump but no more than a bruise or two. My patient is Felix Brabant. He's French, forty-three years old. He was heading for New

Caledonia but got blown off course by the storm. He has a dislocated shoulder, a dislocation fracture of his elbow and a compound radial fracture. I've splinted everything as best I can and given him pain relief. He's pretty drowsy now but his GCS was good enough to talk me through getting the engines going.'

It was the pilot who took over the radio now.

'Are you able to follow us back to port? There's a tricky gap through the reef to navigate. Over...'

'I'm no sailor but I can follow directions. And I should warn you that I have no experience of navigating reefs.' Lia sounded less sure of herself. 'Over...'

'Stand by, Lia. We'll sort this out. Over...'

The men looked at each other. Transferring anyone between boats in these conditions would be difficult. Getting someone who was badly injured and now medicated to the point of being unable to help himself was going to make it even more dangerous.

'Put me on board,' Sam said. 'I need to check that the engine's powerful enough. If it's not, we'll have to transfer them and ditch the boat. If it is, I can bring the yacht in. We'll head for Wildfire and get them straight up to the hospital. You can take Jack back to Atangi to collect the chopper.'

The pilot pressed the transmission button on the microphone. 'Lia? We're going to get right alongside and Sam's going to come on board to take you in. Come up on deck. We'll need you to catch a rope. Over...'

'On my way. Over and out.'

It took more than one attempt and all the pilot's skill to get the buffered edges of the coastguard launch touching the yacht and keeping it there for more than a split second. The jump between boats was a hair-raising moment but in the end Sam didn't actually need the rope that Lia had been about to tether to the yacht because he jumped at the same instant the launch bumped against the yacht and he jumped as if he had wings on his feet.

He landed with a lurch that sent him barrelling into Lia. She tried to break his momentum by putting her arms out but they both hit the deck.

And there they were. On a slippery deck in a fading storm, wrapped in each other's arms, and they were grinning at each other.

They could hear the roar of the launch moving away but they didn't stop grinning. Or look up. Sam couldn't tear his gaze away from Lia's eyes.

He had never felt like this in his life.

His words came out without him even thinking about what he was saying. The feeling was so huge, it had to escape.

'I love you,' he growled. 'Don't you ever give me a fright like this again.'

Lia's eyes widened. Her mouth opened and then closed. Her eyes crinkled as if she was trying not to cry and her lips wobbled as she tried to smile.

'I love you, too.'

Could there ever have been a less appropriate moment to exchange such life-changing declarations? They were still in trouble. They had to get this damaged vessel back to a safe port and they had a patient below deck that needed their help.

They had only been lying on the deck like that for a matter of seconds but it was time to move. Whatever had just happened would have to be put on hold. Sam struggled to his feet and held out his hands to help Lia up. Was this just a heat-of-the-moment thing? A reaction to the relief of him finding that Lia was uninjured and Lia now having someone to help her back to safety?

Maybe when this was over things would change and they might both be embarrassed by what had been said.

But Lia was gripping his hands and, as she regained her footing, her gaze was holding Sam's and he knew…

He knew that nothing would change.

This was as real as it got.

CHAPTER EIGHT

PICKING UP THE pieces always took so much longer than the event that had caused them.

And coping with that process could seem harder at times. The adrenaline rush of trying to survive was long gone and the relief of succeeding was also wearing off. Now was the time to count the cost. To survey the damage and put plans into action that would help people rebuild their lives and eventually reinstate the normality everybody longed for. Now, two days after the worst of the storm had passed over them, there was time to collate all the information they had and assign priorities.

Sam, on behalf of the medical team, and Ky, as the chief of police and civil defence on the main island of Atangi, had met in the hospital staffroom to do exactly that.

Cyclones were nothing new around here and Sam had done this before. He knew how hard these days of picking up the pieces could be and the strain of it all was evident on Ky's face but, for him personally, it was very different this time.

There was the same kind of destruction to be found in these islands he loved, of course—houses with roofs torn off, trees uprooted, boats that hadn't been as lucky as his own and had been bashed against rocks and destroyed. There was too much work to do and not enough manpower to do it quickly. The hospital was full to bursting, thanks to the damage to one wing that had taken some bed space away, and there were people who had been seriously injured, like Hika and the French yachtsman, Felix. Sam was worried about Sefina, too, who had spiked a temperature and would need watching in case she had an infection brewing. Yes. He was worried and tired and sad for people who had lost important things.

But he was also happier than he had ever been in his life.

Because he was in love.

And Lia had said that she loved him back…

Not that they'd had the time to celebrate this miracle that had happened in the middle of the total chaos of the cyclone. There'd been the scary time of getting the crippled yacht back into port and then many, many hours spent in surgery with Felix to try and save his arm.

Yesterday Sam had barely caught sight of Lia as she and Jack had taken the helicopter to every inhabited island in the area. They had done an aerial survey to check for serious damage to dwellings and then landed to check, treat and transport anybody who needed help. Now they had a good idea of what they were dealing with over the whole spread of this chain of islands that was M'Langi, and this was what he and Ky had been discussing.

'We were so lucky that the cyclone changed direction when it did and went back out to sea. Seems like it was only the northern end of Atangi that got really clipped. That's where the real structural damage to houses is concentrated.'

'It's great to know that the outer islands are okay.'

Sam nodded. 'There's minor damage. Roofs lifted but not ripped off. Trees down and crops ruined. A few injuries but nothing that needed transporting, according to Lia. I've got the list of people she saw and treated here…'

'I saw the chopper every time I looked up yesterday. Even out at night, with the light going. Those guys must have been exhausted by the time they stopped, I reckon. I hope they both got a good sleep last night.'

He could imagine Lia asleep in her bed, with those long limbs completely relaxed. Did she tie her hair up at night or did it spread out like a soft, dark wave over her pillows? A wave of longing washed through him. He wished he'd been there with her. Holding her in his arms. But he'd been on duty in the intensive care unit, monitoring Felix and Hika, occasionally snatching a bit of sleep on one of the comfortable armchairs here in the staffroom.

Maybe tonight he could be holding Lia. And that would be after they'd made love…

Oh, man…it was a bit of an effort to shake that train of thought back to where it belonged, which was out of work hours.

'You're looking a bit tired yourself, Ky.'

The big police officer smiled. 'I might get some sleep tonight. Last night I got a call from someone who'd spotted Louis Dason. I'd put the word out that I wanted to find him. We got a team together and went hunting for a few hours but…' He shrugged, shaking his head.

'No luck?'

'Nah… He's gone to ground somewhere and it's going to be easy enough to hide for the next few days. There's a lot of houses that have been abandoned until they can get fixed. And that's where the manpower has to go for the moment. We can't waste time searching for someone who doesn't want to be found. I've got anybody with any trade skills in building and plumbing sorted into teams and we've got a list we're working through one at a time. We'll be looking after some families in the school hall for a few days longer.' He glanced up at Sam. 'How's Sefina doing?'

'The surgery went well. We'll be keeping her in a while longer, though. She's running a bit of a temperature today.'

'Has she said anything about Louis?'

'She won't talk about it. Won't change her story. Not officially, anyway. I think she might have said something to Hettie. I don't think she realises how obvious it is that those injuries couldn't have been caused by a fall.'

'We'll find him,' Ky vowed. 'And ship him off to the mainland. Hopefully they'll lock him up and throw away the key.'

'It won't happen without a statement from Sefina. I'll see if Hettie can persuade her.'

'How's the kid?'

'See for yourself.' Sam could see the doorway behind Ky, where two women were coming into the staffroom.

Hettie had Joni in her arms. Lia was right behind her, cradling a well-wrapped baby.

'This place is turning into a creche.' But Sam couldn't have been happier to see the children arriving, given who had come with them. His gaze met Lia's and was caught. Never mind working hours—there was no way he could simply make polite eye contact and look away again.

He could spend the rest of his life looking into those eyes. Feeling that connection that went straight to his soul. Revelling in the knowledge that it would be possible to find limitless strength in that connection. Ultimate comfort. And a desire the likes of which he hadn't known existed.

It was just as well nobody else seemed to have noticed.

'Need some help?' Ky stood up to ruffle Joni's curls. He tickled the small boy, who giggled. 'We've got lots of kids being looked after in the school hall. One more wouldn't make any difference.'

'No.' Hettie looked alarmed. 'We're doing just fine. Sefina needs to see him every day.' She moved away from Ky to sit on one of the armchairs in the room. 'And we love Joni, don't we?' The question was directed at the toddler, who wrapped his arms around Hettie's neck in response. She kissed his head and answered her query herself in the kind of sing-song voice that came automatically from adults who loved the child they were speaking to. 'Yes, we do…'

Lia was smiling as she sat on the other armchair, adjusting the bundle in her arms. 'Jack's up at the airstrip. He's ready to take you back to Atangi anytime, Ky.'

'I think we're about done. You happy, Sam?'

Sam was still watching Lia, who was still smiling. He smiled back as her eyes met his again. Even with a break of only a second or two, finding that connection was still there gave him a jolt of sheer joy. Would it wear off when he'd met her gaze for the millionth time? It didn't feel like it would.

'Oh, yeah…I'm happy…'

Ky looked from Sam to Lia and then back again. He cleared his throat as if dismissing something he'd seen as being none of his business.

'Do you need me to send a team over from Atangi to deal with repairs here?'

'I don't think so. We've boarded up some windows but the main problem is water damage. Things need to dry out before we can assess what we need to replace. The windows can wait. There are people out there who need help first.'

Ky nodded. He looked at Lia again. 'Who's this little one?'

'She's Hika and Afi's baby.'

'Oh…of course.' Ky's breath came out in an impressed huff. 'Man, you guys did an awesome job there the other night. You're a legend in these parts now, Lia.'

'I was just doing my job.'

Sam shook his head. 'Hardly.' He nodded at Ky. 'She's awesome, all right.'

'Oh, stop…' But Lia's cheeks had gone pink and she seemed to find it necessary to rearrange the folds of muslin around the baby's face.

'Is Afi still here? I've got his house at the top of the list for today. We've got a big team ready to see what they can do.'

'No. He took Ema and Rua back yesterday. Someone said they'd be at the school hall.'

'I'll find him, then. He'll want to be part of the team. How's Hika doing?'

'Really well,' Sam told him. 'She'll be with us for a while, though. And we'll keep the baby with her.'

'And what about the guy from that yacht?'

'Felix?' Sam frowned. 'He might well need some more specialist surgery to make sure he regains full use of his arm but there's no point in evacuating him yet. I spoke to the chief of orthopaedics in Brisbane first thing this morning. We're going to have to wait until the swelling goes down before anything else can be done and that could take a week. He's comfortable.'

'You've got enough space? We've got a flight coming in with supplies later today. Or tomorrow. They're getting the tail end of the weather over the mainland still.'

'We'll manage. There's a few people that can probably go home today, if they've got homes to go back to.'

'Hettie?' Another person appeared at the door. 'We need you. Drug round.'

'Oh...okay...I'll be there in a sec, Matt.' Hettie gave Joni another cuddle before turning her head towards Lia. 'Can he stay here with you for a bit?'

'Sure. If I get a call I'll take him to Vailea.'

Joni wriggled happily into the small space beside Lia on the armchair and somehow she managed to put an arm around the little boy without disrupting the sleeping baby in her arms.

'I'd better go, too,' Ky said. He shook Sam's hand. 'I'll be in touch later to check how things are going but I reckon we're through the worst of this. Good job.'

'And you.'

There was a long moment's silence as Sam and Lia

were left alone in the staffroom together, their eye contact saying things that had been hovering, unspoken, while others had been present and they hadn't been able to sink into this new, wonderful connection they'd discovered.

Huge things.

But Sam didn't even try to say any of them out loud. Instead, he let his gaze rest on Lia and the small people she had gathered to her body.

Something weird was happening in his head. A bit of a time warp, maybe. A flash forward in time that made him realise what it could be like to see Lia with a different baby and toddler in her arms.

Their children?

Holy heck…a week ago a thought like that would have made him break out in a cold sweat. Taking him back to a place he'd sworn he'd never go again.

But this couldn't be more different.

Even his smile felt different. Tender enough to match the lump in his throat.

'Suits you,' he murmured.

Lia grinned. 'I love kids,' she said. 'The more the merrier. Big families are the best.'

The moment the words had left her mouth Lia kicked herself mentally.

She'd been lost in the warmth of the gaze she'd been basking in. The sheer delight in knowing that what had happened between them on the deck of that broken yacht was still there.

Growing, even.

They hadn't had even a few minutes alone together

since then and she'd needed this confirmation as much as she needed her next breath.

But they weren't exactly alone now, were they? She had a tiny baby in her arms and a wriggly toddler on one side. And she'd just told Sam that big families were the best.

She could hear an echo of his voice in her head.

Closest I've come to a family is looking after a borrowed dog.

Did he even know what it was like to have a family? Had he been a lonely child? Was he lonely now?

Lia's heart was breaking. She wanted to add Sam to the pile of humanity in her arms. She wanted to hold him close to her heart and never let him go.

To make him a part of *her* family.

He was already, as far as her heart was concerned.

'Hey…'

'Hey, what?' Sam didn't seem to have been hurt by her careless words. He was still smiling. A smile that was so tender she could imagine exactly what it would be like if she was sitting here holding *his* baby.

Lia didn't bother checking that no one was coming into the room who could overhear but she did keep her voice to a whisper.

'I love you.'

Sam's chair scraped as he pushed it back. Lia's heart picked up speed as he moved towards her and it skipped a beat as he bent his head.

He didn't have to say it back. The words were written all over his face. She could feel them in the way his hands touched her face. She was living them as his lips covered hers in a kiss that blew that gorgeous smile out of the water as far as tenderness went.

And then he said it anyway.

'I love you, too.'

It was Joni who broke the moment. He tugged at Lia's arm.

'Ithe cream,' he said, with an adorable lisp. 'Pleathe?'

'I'd better go and find Vailea.'

'And I'd better do my ward round.' Sam's smile was cheeky now. 'What are you doing after work?'

'I get the afternoon off, apparently. Unless there's an emergency. But the cell phone coverage is up and running again. As long as I don't go too far away, I'm as free as a bird. How 'bout you?'

'I think I can arrange a bit of time off.'

Her breath caught as she imagined what they could do with that bit of time. Private time. In Sam's bedroom, hopefully. But there was something Lia hadn't seen in his eyes before. Something serious? Wary, almost.

'There's something I'd like to show you.'

It was something important. Instinct told her that he was inviting her into a part of his life that he didn't show to many people. This was about something private.

Lia had to swallow past a sudden tightening in her throat. And breathe past the same sensation in her chest.

'I'd like to see it,' she said softly.

'It's a short boat ride away. Want me to check with Jack that it's okay for you to be that far away?'

'I can do that. I need to take some supplies up to the chopper after I've handed over these creche responsibilities.'

'Come back soon.' Sam ducked his head and kissed her again.

He lifted Joni out of the way to give Lia room to get up. And then he lifted his hand in farewell as he moved towards the door, turning his head to smile once more.

'I'll miss you.'

Lia was smiling, too, as she stood up. But her smile wobbled as she saw Sam disappear.

She was missing him already.

'Are we going out on your yacht?' Down at the harbour on Wildfire Island, the boats were still rocking on their moorings. 'That's it, isn't it? *Surf Song?*'

'It's a she.' Sam's look was stern. 'And, yes, that's her.'

Lia remembered what Jack had said. 'The love of your life…'

'She *was*…'

The stern look vanished from Sam's face to be replaced by one that was very different. One that made Lia's heart feel so full it could burst at any moment. The very next beat, probably.

This was crazy. They'd only met a week ago. Only realised that how they felt about each other was mutual a couple of days ago. This couldn't be real, could it? The kind of love that could last a lifetime?

One of her older sisters, Carla, had married young, after only knowing her husband a short time. She and Dino were still happily married with a brood of young children, but there'd been a typical Roselli family ruckus when the engagement and wedding date had been announced back then. Lia could remember the look on Carla's face as she'd made the simple statement that had silenced everybody.

When you know, you just know.

Had Carla felt like this when she'd only been with the man she loved for such a short time?

Lia could certainly believe that.

She knew...Sam was the one for her. The person she could be with—and love—forever.

Okay, there might be a few logistical issues to figure out but she wasn't even going to think about that today.

Not when that look she was basking in from Sam suggested that *he* knew, too.

That this *was* real.

It took her a moment to tune back in to what Sam was saying.

'...so we'll take my motor boat. The seas are still big enough to need a powerful motor to get through the gap in the reef. It'll be like this for days and I wouldn't risk taking *Surf Song* out.'

Holding her hand, he helped Lia onto the small boat moored alongside his yacht.

'It'll be a bit rough but I reckon I know you well enough to know that you quite like a bit of an adrenaline rush. Here, put this on...' He eased a life jacket over her head but he didn't let go of it when it was resting on her shoulders. Instead, he pulled her closer so that only the squashy orange cushions of the jacket separated their bodies. The sea rolled beneath them and he slipped his arms completely around her body to hold her steady. It felt like the most natural thing in the world to lift her own arms and wrap them around Sam's neck. To lift her face and stand on tiptoe so that she could kiss his lips.

It was Sam who broke the kiss.

'Don't start that,' he warned. 'Or we'll never get to where we're going.'

'Where *are* we going?'

'Not far.' The engine of Sam's boat started instantly, with a powerful roar. 'Hold on to your hat.'

Everything about her time here so far had been wild enough to live up to the island's name. From that first flight in on the fixed-wing aircraft to the helicopter trips with Jack. And the work had been something she'd be telling stories about for the rest of her career. Crawling beneath the wreckage of a house. Getting dropped onto a crippled yacht and being abandoned in a terrifyingly huge sea.

Maybe the wildest story of all—and the one she would be telling her grandchildren—would end up being that she'd found the love of her life in the midst of all that adventure and danger.

This short boat ride might still be wild but it wasn't dangerous. Sam knew how to handle the boat and he'd been right, they weren't going far. Straight out from the western side of Wildfire to one of the many dots that were the uninhabited islands sprinkled right through this archipelago.

This one had a deep cleft in its shoreline, with only a narrow entranceway, but then it opened out to a small but astonishingly pretty tree-lined beach. The water was almost smooth in here, thanks to the protection of the wings of this island.

A jetty had been built to one side of the beach and it was easy enough to climb out without help. Lia looked around as she reached the end of the jetty. The only sign of the cyclone here were the coconuts and driftwood littering the pure, white sand of the beach. This was clearly a safe place to be but why had Sam brought her here?

'What's the name of this island? Who lives here?'

'It doesn't have a name yet. And no one lives here. Yet.'

'But there's a jetty. And…and is that a house?' Lia shaded her eyes with her hand as the sun broke through the heavy cloud cover for a moment. 'I can see something…up there in the forest.'

'It's a work in progress,' Sam told her. 'I needed to check that everything's still okay after the storm.'

So somebody was building a house on a tiny, private patch of tropical paradise. Lia followed Sam up a track that wound its way past huge tree trunks and tangles of vines. A flock of startled parrots took wing, chiding them for the disturbance.

The house was well under way. The foundations were complete and the framework of the walls in place.

'Kind of lucky the roof wasn't on yet, I guess.' Sam was testing the framework as he walked slowly around the construction site. 'This all seems as solid as a rock. I'll get hold of Pita later and tell him he's doing a good job.'

'Pita?'

'He lives on Atangi. He was the foreman of the crew that built the conference centre on Wildfire. They were all a bit short of work when that project got finished. He's a great builder.'

'From what I've heard, there'll be more work than all the builders here can keep up with for a while.'

'True. I'll remind him that there's no rush to come back here.' Sam smiled at Lia. 'Do you like it?'

'This house? The island? What's not to like?' From this high point of the small island, Lia could see over the trees below to the cleft of the island's shape and farther, to where Wildfire Island was sitting directly in front of them.

'Look at the shape of this island. It's like folded angel's wings.'

'It is.' Sam was staring down at the wings of land. 'How 'bout that for a name? Angel Island.'

'I just named an island? How cool. You might have to run that one past Pita.'

'I'll do that.' But Sam was looking beyond the foreshore now. 'We're facing Sunset Beach. You know, the one where you were playing windmills just before the cyclone hit?'

Lia grinned at him. How could she forget that? The place they'd had their first kiss that had unlocked the passion they'd gone on to explore in Sam's bed. And, as huge as that passion had been, it seemed less powerful than this new depth of feeling she'd found for Sam.

The love that could last a lifetime.

'You haven't seen what happens on that beach, thanks to the weather since you got here, but it gets its name from the way the cliffs glow like they're on fire at sunset. It's where the name of the whole island comes from.'

'It sounds gorgeous. I want to see that.'

'This will be the best place of all to see it from. There's going to be a big deck coming out from this living area and it'll be a front-row seat to the greatest show on earth.'

Lia turned from the view to meet Sam's gaze. The logistical issues were rushing up at her. Would she be here to see one of those sunsets when the sky cleared completely? She was due to be back on the mainland in a week's time.

She had her family there and they needed her. How soon would she be able to get back to Sam? How often?

She couldn't say anything about it. Not yet. Not when this was the first time they'd been alone together since they'd declared their love for each other. This was too new. Too precious to risk putting obstacles in its path.

And wasn't it a bit premature to be worrying about the future when she still had so much to learn about this man she'd fallen in love with?

'I don't even know where you're from.' The words tumbled out unexpectedly. 'What made you come here in the first place and if this is where you want to be forever. I love you, Sam, but I don't really know anything about you. Is that crazy?'

'Probably.' But Sam was smiling as he pulled Lia into his arms. 'I don't know much about you, either, but this feels so…right. As if I've been waiting my whole life to find you.'

This time they didn't kiss. Lia kept her head nestled against Sam's shoulder, loving the feel of his arms around her.

'I don't even know if you're single,' she murmured. 'You could be married.' Her head jerked up. '*Are* you married?'

'Not anymore.'

Lia gasped. 'You *have* been married?' It felt like she'd been doused with a bucket of icy water.

Sam sighed. 'Come on, it's a bit windy up here. Let

me show you the beach and I'll tell you anything you want to know.'

So Lia asked him questions as they made their way down the track and onto the white sands of the beach. She learned that he had grown up in the north of England. That he'd done his training in Birmingham and had gone on to specialise in intensive care medicine. That he'd married a nurse who'd worked in that unit because he'd thought he was in love.

Thought?

Did that mean he knew he hadn't really been in love?

Because he now knew what that *really* felt like?

They'd got to the end of the beach before Lia learned why Sam had walked away from his previous life and career.

'Vicky told me she was pregnant and I was over the moon. I was going to be a father.'

They were sitting on a huge driftwood log by now and Lia was holding Sam's hand. She knew there was something awful he was about to tell her. A dreadful accident, perhaps, that had torn his wife and unborn baby from his life?

'I wasn't the father,' Sam continued. 'Turned out that the father of her baby was another doctor in the unit. My best friend.'

'Oh, my God…' Lia breathed. 'How could she have done that?' She let go of Sam's hand to touch his face. How could any woman have done something like that to Sam? How could this Vicky have not known she had been the luckiest woman in the world with what she already had?

He must have been able to see her total lack of comprehension in her eyes. And maybe the reason behind it—that she could never even contemplate doing something like that to the man she loved.

I'm not like that, her touch was telling him. *I love you. You can trust me.*

Sam caught her hand and pressed his lips to it, seemingly lost for words.

'I'm not surprised you left. Nobody could live with that being rubbed in day after day.'

'I felt like a complete idiot,' Sam admitted. 'It felt like everybody had known she'd never actually loved me. That I'd been taken for a ride.' He sighed heavily. 'I took leave. I intended to go back but I needed a break. I took *Surf Song* and sailed off. By chance, I ended up here and they were short of a doctor at the hospital. The rest, as they say, is history. It didn't happen overnight but I'd found the place in the world I most wanted to be. I love these islands. I love the people. And...and I make a real difference to their lives. It goes both ways.'

'Haven't you been lonely?'

'I was going to get a dog.' There was a gleam in Sam's eyes that suggested he needed to lighten the atmosphere. 'But now I've found you...'

That drew another gasp from Lia. 'Cheers,' she told him. '*Not*...' But she was smiling. She knew what he was really trying to say—that he might never be lonely again because he'd found *her*...

'It's your turn,' Sam said. 'Are you married?'

'Nope. Never got close. I've been too wrapped up in my career and I never met the right person...'

The pause seemed too significant. As if she'd left off the end of that sentence.

Until now.

'Plus, I have a family the size of Africa,' Lia added quickly. 'They take all my spare time. Especially Angel.'

'Angel?'

'My niece. She's six. She was born prematurely with cerebral palsy. Her father walked out as soon as he knew she was disabled. My sister couldn't manage by herself and moved back home a while ago. I moved back, too, to help out.' She smiled at Sam. 'It's tough but I wouldn't have it any other way. She's the most adorable kid and I love her to bits.'

'What will she think when she knows there's an island named after her?'

'Do you think Pita will like the name?'

'Doesn't matter if he doesn't. It's *my* island.'

'What?'

Sam shrugged. 'It's no big deal. The local government needed to raise some funds a couple of years back and someone came up with the idea of selling one of the islands. They used the money to build the community hall by the school—the one that the people are living in now until their houses get fixed. It wasn't that expensive compared to land anywhere in England, that's for sure.'

'Really?' Lia thought of her parents and the worry in their faces when they'd been talking about how to make the mortgage payments on their house when the redundancy money ran out. Maybe they could think of moving somewhere where the land was cheaper. Here, even? The thought was ridiculous. Or was it?

'I hadn't been planning to build a house on it,' Sam continued. 'It was just a nice place to come when I wanted a bit of time to myself. But then the work on the conference centre finished and people needed jobs.'

And he'd found a way to provide them. On top of already making a huge contribution to the community he'd made his home in.

Lia's heart squeezed. She'd learned a lot about Sam today. She already knew that he'd been without a real family and had probably been a lonely child. He'd been badly hurt by the betrayal of his wife and his best friend. And he was generous towards the people he cared about.

Love could keep growing, couldn't it? Could develop layer upon layer that made it deeper and stronger.

It was Lia's turn to be lost for words. She had to turn away from the compassion in Sam's eyes before her own filled up with tears and overflowed, which could well spoil the moment. Instead, she looked at the beach. Even now, with the sea still wild out in the open, there were only baby waves lapping against the sand here.

Angel loved the water. She loved the beach but the surf around Brisbane was too big for her to ever be able to swim in the sea. Imagine if she could come here for a holiday and play in these wavelets? Move her body in water that was warm enough to stay in for as long as you wanted?

But to live here in this isolated patch of the Pacific? Away from her family?

How could she do that?

The touch of Sam's hand made her turn her head again. The touch of his lips against hers reminded her of how private this beach was. This kiss wasn't going to stop anytime soon.

And Lia didn't want it to. She wanted to make love with Sam right here, under the palm trees that bordered this gorgeous little island.

Sam's island.

How could she leave her family behind to live here?

Sinking into the kiss and letting herself get swept away by the passion, Lia only had one more coherent thought.

How could she not live here, if it meant she could be with Sam forever?

CHAPTER NINE

MAYBE THERE WERE only brief glimpses of the sun between the big, fluffy clouds this morning but it had never shone so brightly.

Sam had to shade his eyes with his hand as he stepped outside his cabin to walk to work the next morning.

It could be that the sunshine and the warmth of the day seemed more astonishing than usual because it was such a contrast to the dark side of the weather that had been around them for the past few days.

Or it could be that he was seeing life through the eyes of a man in love, and everything—including the weather—was simply perfect.

Too good to be true?

What a difference a day could make. Well, a day and night, actually.

Making love to Lia in the absolute privacy of his own island had been amazing. A confirmation of everything he'd seen in her eyes when he'd told her his story and she'd been so horrified that anyone could have done what Vicky had done to him. A physical expression of the promise he'd seen—that Lia could never do something like that to the man she loved.

And he *was* that man…

Neither of them had noticed that the surroundings weren't that ideal for that kind of intimacy but it wasn't until they'd come home and showered off the sand and then started all over again in the comfort of his bed that they realised how much better it *could* be.

Lia had gone back to her own accommodation to find a clean uniform and tidy up for work so Sam was left with a bit of time on his own to contemplate the contrasts that made life so wonderful.

Cyclones and sunshine.

Loneliness and love…

While it wasn't something he would have chosen to do, it was inevitable that Sam was making contrasts between Vicky and Lia, too. He'd never talked about his past life with anyone here because it was something he had chosen to move on from and try to forget. Talking about it had made a lot of memories resurface.

Bitter, hurtful memories. How good was it that he could superimpose memories of Lia on top of them?

There'd never been that kind of connection in working together that made him feel like he had another pair of hands that he could trust as much as his own.

Sex had never been so astonishing. So much more than a physical pleasure and release.

And Vicky had never looked at him the way Lia had yesterday. As if all the love in the world had collected in her eyes and could be freely given in no more than a glance.

He'd spent months with Vicky before deciding that this was the woman he wanted to marry and spend the rest of his life with.

Was he completely crazy to be thinking that it was

really true about Lia when he'd only known her a matter of days?

No, not thinking…

Knowing.

He probably had a goofy smile on his face as he walked through the garden to gain entrance to the hospital building.

Life was good. And it would get even better soon, because the plane from the mainland was due to arrive and Lia was going to collect the new supplies they'd been waiting for since the cyclone had disrupted normal routines, and bring them down to the hospital.

Maybe things would have calmed down around here enough for him to take a quick break. To sit in the garden with Lia, perhaps, and bask in a bit more of what her eyes could tell him.

It was too soon to tell her how permanent he wanted this to be but he could dream a little, couldn't he?

He had a few more steps before he had to enter his place of work and turn his focus to his patients and he would have been happy to use that for daydreaming. The ringing of his mobile phone seemed a rude interruption until he saw who the caller was.

'Pita…I was going to call you today. I went out to the house yesterday. It's looking great. I can't see any significant damage from the weather.'

He listened for a few moments. 'Of course…I understand. You must have a lot on at the moment. There's no rush to get back to my job. I…' His jaw dropped as he had to stop speaking to listen again. '*What...?*'

Ending the call, he moved swiftly towards the staffroom. Jack was sitting beside the radio, scribbling in a logbook.

'Hey, Sam. Gorgeous day, isn't it? Those clouds will be gone in no time. We could fly anywhere.'

'Yeah…it's going to be hot.' Sam reached past Jack to shift some books and journals. 'Did you see a white envelope here? Pita came in last night to collect it and says it wasn't here.'

'Nope.' Jack glanced at his watch. 'I'd better go. I said I'd collect Lia in the golf cart and get her up to the airfield to collect the supplies. I need to do a thorough check on the chopper. She's been put through her paces the last few days, that's for sure.' He glanced back at Sam, who was still shuffling through the piles of paper and files that seemed to always collect on the radio desk. 'How long ago did you leave it there?'

'Must be at least a week. It was…' Sam frowned. He could remember putting the cash in the envelope. Pushing the envelope into his pocket. A big pocket. Oh, yeah…he'd been wearing that white coat.

'It was Lia's first day at work.'

Because he'd put that stupid coat on to try and impress her, hadn't he? Even though he'd already written her off after that comment she'd made at the airfield.

Who knew they paid so much more for coming here in the cyclone season?

He could remember the phone call from Pita and telling him where he would leave the envelope, but he couldn't actually remember putting it where he'd said he was going to put it.

Because he'd been distracted, hadn't he? That cardiac arrest in the garden. When he'd worked with Lia and had started to revise his earlier opinion of her. He'd pulled the coat off because it had been hampering his movements. He'd pulled it off, rolled it up and shoved it…

On the bottom level of the resuscitation trolley.

'Never mind,' he told Jack. 'I think I know where it is.'

The trolley hadn't been needed since then. It would be in the storage room near Theatre.

It was. And, yes…the discarded white coat was still a crumpled heap amongst boxes of gloves and bags of saline.

He shook it out and reached into the pockets. So that was where his diary had got to. He'd been hunting for that yesterday morning because he'd needed the dates for the clinics coming up on Atangi and other islands. Important clinics where they were going to be starting trials for the new encephalitis vaccine they had available specifically for these islands.

The reminder came as a jolt. First the cyclone and now Lia. Was he losing focus on what his life was really all about? Not just the career he loved but these islands and these people. *His* people now. His home.

And that reminded him of the house he was building. And that Pita needed to be paid or he wouldn't be able to do any more work on it.

He checked the other pockets. Searched the whole trolley and poked under the shelves in the storage room but there was no sign of the envelope.

Who had put the trolley back in here?

Anahera?

He went to find her.

'Sam…I was going to call you. Can you take a look at Felix? His pain level seems to be increasing and I think the capillary refill in the nails of his injured hand is getting slower.'

'Sure. I'll be there in just a minute. Hey…do you remember the day of Keoni's arrest?'

'Of course.'

'Do you remember who put the resus trolley away in the end?'

Anahera frowned. 'Hmm. It was in the corner of ICU for a while because I put the life pack back on it after we'd switched over the monitoring to the bedside gear. I don't know who put it back in storage, though.'

Lia had been standing in the corner of the ICU, hadn't she? Sending and receiving those text messages that had annoyed him so much. Maybe she would remember.

A junior nurse poked her head around the door.

'Have you seen Sefina?'

'No, why?'

'She told me she was discharging herself this morning. I told her she'd have to wait to see one of the doctors but then I got busy with other patients. And now I can't find her.'

'Maybe she's with Joni. Try the kitchens.' Anahera caught Sam's gaze. 'Can you come and see Felix now?'

'Of course.' With an effort, Sam put the concern of the missing envelope and cash out of his mind and turned his attention to more important things. It had just been misplaced in the chaos of a crisis—that was all. It would turn up.

If it wasn't for the evidence all around her of the very recent cyclone, like bushes having been stripped of their flowers and having to dodge coconuts that hadn't been cleared from the road yet, Lia was finding it increasingly hard to believe it had even happened.

Under the clear, blue sky and sunshine that was gaining warmth by the minute, she drove the little golf cart laden with supplies for the hospital and knew that anybody who saw her would probably think she was crazy—all by herself but with a huge grin on her face.

Because she was driving towards where Sam was.

How different her life felt at this moment was even more unbelievable than how bad the cyclone had been.

This was what it felt like to be in love.

No wonder Carla had declared that when you knew, you just knew. It was *so* true.

And maybe she needed to cut a bit of slack for her younger sister, Elena, who was with the much older boyfriend the entire family had deemed so unsuitable. Maybe she was in love and maybe it was real. She could just imagine her family's reaction when she was home next week and announced that she'd met the man she was going to marry.

Lia actually laughed aloud as she pictured her mother crossing herself or slamming a pot lid and muttering something along the lines of, *Mamma mia, Lia—and I thought you were the sensible one of the family...*

The laughter—and the smile—faded.

The stab of homesickness reminded her of how much she was missing her family. The crowded dinner tables and her mother's wonderful food. Cuddles from Angel. Even the teasing and incessant arguments. They always got resolved in the end because the one thing the Roselli family had in abundance was love.

How was Nico doing now that he'd started his chemo?

And Angel? She was due for an appointment with an orthopaedic specialist down in Brisbane because there'd been discussions that a surgical release of some ligaments and tendons might be necessary to help her walk when those specially designed aids had been made.

The smile reappeared. She would be able to pay for those aids thanks to the bonus she was earning by working here.

And then it faded completely.

On one side of her was the pull of her family and the need to be with them.

But on the other was…Sam.

And these gorgeous islands. His *private* island. Who wouldn't think it was a dream come true to live in a place like this? She wouldn't be short of friends. All the people she'd met so far, like Anahera and Hettie and Caroline and Jack, had the potential to be special people in her life. And the work… Well, she'd had more excitement and used more of her skills in the last week than she would have in a month back home. A year, even. Maybe forever. How many houses got wrecked in cyclones around Brisbane? And even if it did happen, there'd be a queue of highly trained urban search and rescue team members who'd be way ahead of her to get to the action.

Would they want a permanent paramedic on the islands? It might be less expensive for them than adding the travel costs and bonuses of bringing FIFO staff in, especially in the cyclone season.

They could still do that, though. She'd need time off when she had babies…

Whoa...

Who was getting just a little ahead of herself here?

But the grin was back as Lia parked the golf cart outside Wildfire hospital and began to ferry in the cartons of supplies. She knew where some of them needed to go, too. Boxes of IV supplies went to the storeroom near the intensive care unit. New linen went to another storage area. She didn't have a key to get into the drug cupboard, though, so she carried that box to the staffroom to find someone who did.

Hettie was on a day off but Anahera would. Or Caroline. Or...Sam...

He was sitting at the radio desk, a folder open in front of him.

'Hey...'

He looked up and Lia soaked in the way his face changed. The crinkles around his eyes that advertised a smile was on the way. The softening of those eyes that she'd looked into enough that she could describe every tiny detail. Blue-grey, with a darker rim and a ring of hazel around the pupil that was an exact match for the colour of his hair.

She loved those eyes. She loved the floppy hair. She loved the way he could look at her as though the sun was coming out again after a huge storm. A cyclone, even.

'Hey, yourself.' He stood up, abandoning whatever work he was doing, to walk towards her. 'Let me take that.' He reached for the small locked box. 'It's good to see the drugs have arrived.' Taking the box from her arms, he leaned in farther to place a slow kiss on her lips. 'You should have had security riding with you, carrying this lot.'

'It's one of my splinter skills.' Lia grinned. 'I know kung-fu.'

Sam grinned back. 'That wouldn't surprise me in the least. Oh…you don't happen to have a Brisbane Hospital staff directory tucked into that amazing brain of yours, do you? I'm trying to find the number for the guy we spoke to about Felix. I'm not really happy with the amount of pain he's in. Graham somebody, but his surname has fallen out of my head. Keanu took the call and I don't want to disturb him on his day off.'

'Graham Appleby. Professor Appleby, in fact.'

Sam shook his head. 'You really *are* amazing. How on earth did you know that?'

Lia laughed. 'It's more of a coincidence than a miracle. I told you my niece has cerebral palsy. Professor Appleby is one of the members of the multidisciplinary team that manages her problems. He's the best.'

Sam pulled a pen from his pocket and wrote on his hand. 'I'll get hold of him in a minute.' Then he glanced up, an eyebrow raised. 'While I'm picking that astonishing brain of yours, do you remember the first day you worked here? That cardiac arrest?'

'You mean when I got to see what an awesome doctor you were for the first time? When you were trying to impress me by wearing that starched white coat?' Lia's smile was the product of something warm and bubbly inside. Something very tender.

'Exactly. Do you remember that I shoved the coat onto the bottom of the resus trolley?'

'No. But I remember thinking how much better you looked without it. I'd go as far as to say *hot…*'

But Sam was frowning. 'You were standing beside

the trolley in ICU when we were stabilising Keoni. You didn't see an envelope drop off it, did you?'

Lia shook her head. 'What sort of envelope?'

'Small. But quite fat. I'm paying Pita for the work on the house in cash, so he can pay the other guys and suppliers more easily. There was ten thousand dollars in the envelope and it's gone missing.'

Lia's jaw dropped. 'Who has ten thousand dollars to put in an envelope? I knew you were rich but… That's ridiculous, Sam. How could you leave it lying around? Anyone could have taken it.'

The words were so casual.

I knew you were rich...

Part of the blame had to lie with the way his memory had been working this morning, comparing Lia to Vicky. The way stuff that had been buried for so long was too close to the surface now. It was too easy to make a very unwelcome reappearance. Like that gut-wrenching final conversation with his wife. His pregnant wife who had been carrying a baby that wasn't his.

'You said you loved me.' He could still feel the tears choking his words.

'Men are so easy to fool.'

'Why did you marry me?'

'Why do you think, Sam?' The laughter had been unforgettably cruel. *'Everybody knows how rich you are...'*

He kept his voice as neutral as he could. 'What do you mean, you know I'm rich?'

Lia had already been looking shocked. Now her face seemed to freeze and her eyes filled with wariness. Maybe his tone hadn't been as neutral as he'd intended.

'You own an island, for heaven's sake. And a yacht.'

He'd tried to make light of his assets by telling her that land wasn't exorbitantly priced in the islands. Lots of people had yachts. How much did she *really* know?

His stare was clearly making Lia uncomfortable. She looked away and he saw her fingers curl and then straighten.

'And...people have said things. About the way you...um...buy stuff for the hospital when it's needed. About...how generous you are.' She was offering him a small smile. 'It's one of the things I love about you.'

One of the things? There was an evil voice in the back of his head—a gust of bitterness left over from a hurricane of betrayal.

More likely to be the only really *important* thing.

'Money's very important to you, isn't it, Lia?'

'*What?* What's that supposed to mean?'

Good grief...he had said that out loud? Of course he had. Lia was looking bewildered. Hurt. As if he'd slapped her.

It could be guilt, the nasty little voice whispered. *You've found out the truth.*

He could hear echoes of Lia's voice now.

Lucky for me... Who knew they paid so much more for coming here in the cyclone season?

Travelling's never been in my budget. That's why it's so exciting to be here.

He'd felt that knot of tension in his gut when he'd heard that one the first time. He'd actually wondered if it was exciting because Wildfire was an exotic location or whether she was more excited about adding to the reserves in her budget.

She could send any financial woes she might have

packing forever by getting hitched to someone who'd inherited a not insubstantial fortune, couldn't she?

Even half of what was left would set her up for life.

The way it had set up Vicky and the father of her baby...

His mouth seemed to have taken on a life of its own.

'You didn't make any secret of it being why you came here in the first place, did you, Lia? For the money?'

'Are you suggesting that I took *your* money? In the envelope?'

'*No*. Of course I'm not.'

He wasn't. He'd actually completely forgotten about the damned envelope as his mind was dragging him back into the past. He would never have suggested Lia was dishonest—that was unthinkable.

He'd just been sidetracked because of the subject and now they'd come full circle and he could see why she might think that that was what he'd been leading up to. Now his mind was going in crazy circles itself. How could he put this right?

'I'm sorry...I've had stuff on my mind, that's all. And I never wanted anyone to know I was wealthy.' He rubbed his forehead with the heel of his hand. 'I told you about Vicky. That was why *she* married me. The *only* reason...'

Oh, man...this was not the time to be telling Lia the whole sorry saga of his disastrous marriage. He was making things worse. He'd pretty much confessed that he'd been thinking about his ex-wife this morning, which was true but not in the way that Lia looked like she was thinking it was.

She was so pale and still she looked like she could

crumple in a heap at any moment. Fragile would have been the last word he would ever have thought of to describe Lia Roselli but that's how she looked right now.

And he'd dug a huge hole for himself by saying where the cash had been. Right beside Lia. If he tried to take that back would he put his foot in things again, the way he just had?

'You don't trust me.'

The words were a statement, not a question.

'That's not true. I do trust you. I…' He wanted to say *I love you*, but the words somehow got stuck in his head. How could you say those words to someone who was looking at you as if you'd just grown two heads or something? Had become someone—or something—that you would never choose to be near.

To make things worse, Anahera appeared at the staffroom door. 'That morphine top-up doesn't seem to have brought the pain scale down for Felix. Do you want to go ahead with taking his cast off to see what's going on?'

'Yes. I'll put in a call to Brisbane first.' To the specialist whose name he now knew, thanks to Lia.

He turned to face her, as Anahera vanished as swiftly as she'd come. He opened his mouth to say that they'd talk about this later. *Soon.* That he wasn't, in any way, accusing her of anything. That he never would.

But he didn't get the chance.

'This was never real, was it, Sam?' Her voice had a hollow tone to it. As if it was a ghost of Lia speaking, not the real woman standing in front of him. 'This…' she made a movement with her hands '…whatever we thought we had.' Her eyes looked as haunted as her voice sounded. '*None* of it was real.'

She left the room as swiftly as Anahera had. As if she were on a mission that someone's life depended on.

Her own?

CHAPTER TEN

TEARS BLURRED LIA'S vision so much that the islands were no more than green smudges on a blue background.

A week ago she would have declared that she never cried. That she could cope with whatever life threw at her and she was far more familiar with mopping up other people's tears than her own. She was the strongest person in her family—everyone knew that. She was the one they all relied on for any medical advice. The one who provided the reassurance and encouragement anyone needed when they were sick or worried. The one who'd given up her independent life and moved home to help with the enormous amount of time and effort and energy it took to raise a disabled child.

But how often had she cried in the last week, for heaven's sake?

Down on the beach that time, when she'd had to tell Sam why she'd been so unprofessional and texting on her phone all day and the pent-up anxiety and guilt and relief about not being there for Nico's surgery had come bubbling out.

And when she'd been so exhausted in the wake of

the worst of the cyclone and rescuing Hika from her crushed home and homesickness had kicked in.

She'd almost cried yesterday, too, when Sam had been telling her his story and she'd realised how lonely he must have been as a child and how devastated he would have been by the betrayal of the woman he'd married. Her heart had been breaking for the boy and the man she hadn't even known.

Was that what the trigger always was? The link with family and love?

But here she was, crying again. Because she was on her way to seeing her family again?

Or were these angry tears perhaps, because she'd run away from something she should have been able to cope with?

But it had all happened so fast.

How kind had Jack been when she'd arrived back at the airfield with the golf cart, having fled from Sam's horrible accusations? That she was just like his ex-wife and only interested in his money. That she had taken the envelope with a stupid amount of cash in it.

Jack had taken one look at her face and known something was horribly wrong. Because he knew about Nico, he assumed she'd been contacted because of a family emergency and Lia hadn't tried to correct the assumption. It had *felt* like a personal emergency.

The supply plane had been about to take off, its engines already running. Jack had signalled the pilot and all but pushed Lia on board the small plane.

'But I'm here to work. You need a crew.'

'I'll use Anahera if we get a call. That's what we always do if there's no paramedic available. We've coped before. We'll cope now. Go. Your family needs you. And that's where *you* need to be.'

'But…' Her protest was weaker this time. The idea of escaping the whole island was so appealing—even more powerful than the force that had driven her so swiftly out of the staffroom—to get away from the devastating realisation that what she had thought she'd found with Sam Taylor was no more than an illusion.

Wishful thinking…

He thought she had fallen in love with him simply because he was rich?

No, it was worse than that. He thought she was *pretending* to be in love with him. Like Vicky had? That she was so obsessed with money she could have *stolen* from him…

'I'll send your stuff on the next plane,' he told her. 'Or maybe you can come back in a day or two.'

Come back?

Not likely.

Lia blinked back her tears and her vision cleared as the plane finished banking and settled onto a straight path. A track that was taking her home.

To her family. Where she belonged.

How had she ever thought she could move away from her home town to live in an isolated collection of Pacific islands?

It would never have worked.

Sam was a loner.

And she couldn't survive without the love of her family.

She needed it now, more than ever. Not that she would be confessing how stupid she'd been, thinking she'd found the person she wanted to spend the rest of her life with. It was cringe-worthy, remembering how sure she'd been.

When you know, you just know.

Her breath came out in an incredulous huff. She wouldn't be subscribing to that belief again anytime soon.

It shouldn't have happened but at least it was over. Lia blinked again and tuned in to the radio conversation the pilot was having. He noticed her glance and raised an eyebrow.

Lia nodded. 'Sounds great.'

There weren't many seats available on connecting flights that could take her from where they were going to land in Cairns back to Brisbane. She'd have a wait of a few hours but the pilot was talking to someone who'd found a gap and would hold a seat for her.

She'd be less than an hour's drive from home when she finally got to Brisbane.

And she still had a couple of hours' flying time before they got to Cairns. Plenty of time to think up a plausible reason for arriving home without her luggage. It had been a last-minute opportunity, perhaps. They didn't need her now that the crisis of the cyclone was over and available flights were few and far between. She'd had the choice of grabbing a seat and having her stuff sent later or waiting a week to come home.

She hadn't been able to wait. That was close enough to the truth, wasn't it?

Getting the cast off Felix's arm had to be done with meticulous care, given the degree of injury it was protecting, but it had to be done because the Frenchman's level of pain suggested that he might be developing compartment syndrome, and if that wasn't dealt with urgently, he could lose the use of his arm and hand permanently. Or lose his arm, even.

It took time. And then it took more time to get in touch with Professor Appleby in Brisbane and discuss what was going on.

Finally, Sam picked up the phone again. This time it was to call Jack.

'Is that supply plane still here?'

'Long gone, I'm afraid.'

'Can we get it to turn around? I've got a patient who needs evacuation to Brisbane urgently.'

'No can do, mate. They wouldn't have enough fuel on board. Want me to activate a rescue plane from Cairns?'

'Yeah… Tell them we'll only need a pilot, though. I want to travel with this guy myself and keep an eye on him.'

'No problem. I'll do that right now.'

'Thanks.'

'And Sam, while I've got you on the phone, can you let Anahera know that I'll need her on call in case we get a chopper mission?'

'What?' It took a sharp shake of his head for Sam to shift his attention from the problem he was already dealing with. 'Where's Lia?'

'She's long gone, too.'

'Sorry?' Surely he hadn't heard that correctly. 'What did you say?'

'I sent her off with the supply plane. She said she had some family emergency going on.'

Sam was stunned into silence. This was totally unexpected. Unbelievable, even.

It was also totally unprofessional. She was upset about something that he'd said so she'd just run away? Lied in order to find an excuse?

Or did she really have a family emergency? The last time he'd thought of her as being unprofessional had been when she'd been doing all that texting about her brother Nico, who had cancer and was just starting his first round of chemotherapy. Had something gone wrong?

At precisely the same time as he'd inadvertently accused her of stealing his money?

That would be a bit far-fetched.

Ending his call to Jack, Sam found himself pacing the staffroom.

No. What was really far-fetched was thinking that a meaningful relationship could have magically appeared in the form of a FIFO medic. There hadn't been anything real there. Not for Lia, anyway. She'd said so—right before she'd run away.

How could he have been so stupid?

He'd broken the rule and he deserved whatever consequences came from it, but he wasn't going to waste any more time thinking about it right now. He had too much to do.

Striding from the staffroom, he went in search of Anahera. He found her outside chatting to Manu, the hospital porter, who was raking up some of the debris the cyclone had left behind in the garden.

'We need to get another cast back on Felix. There's a plane being dispatched from Cairns and I want him ready for transport and up at the airfield, waiting for it.'

'I'll get set up.'

'Get Caroline to help, too. Jack wants you on standby in case there's a chopper callout.'

'What?' Anahera's eyes widened. 'What's happened to Lia? Is she sick?'

'No. Gone. That's something else. Can you find someone to pack her things and take the bag up to the airfield? We're going to drop that at Brisbane Hospital, as well, so she can pick it up sometime.'

'I don't understand…' Anahera was looking shocked. 'What's happened?'

'Family emergency, apparently.' Sam was turning away. He had to step around Manu, who was scooping up leaves to put in his wheelbarrow now.

'What's *that*?' Thankfully, Anahera seemed to have been distracted from asking any further questions about Lia. She moved past Sam and pushed her hand into the pile of damp leaves in the wheelbarrow. 'Look…this isn't that envelope you were looking for, is it?'

Soggy but still intact, it was indeed the envelope. Sam took it from Anahera. The ink of Pita's name had run in the rain, as if someone had been holding it and crying.

And all Sam could think about was the look on Lia's face when he'd said that horrible thing…

You didn't make any secret of it being why you came here in the first place, did you, Lia? For the money?

He'd screwed up. He'd hurt Lia and he felt sick about it.

It didn't matter that his past had programmed him to be suspicious. Lia was as different from Vicky as it was possible to be, but his brain had somehow ignored that fact and let his mouth run away with itself.

Consequences were circling like vultures and would descend to pick at his flesh as soon as he didn't have something concrete to hold up as a barrier, but he did have something.

A patient who needed a great deal of care if he wasn't going to lose an unacceptable degree of his quality of life.

It was later, as the plane took off from Wildfire Island, that Sam realised there would only be a certain number of times he could take his patient's blood pressure and check the limb baselines on his injured arm. There was going to be way too much time for his thoughts to head to where they were so determined to go.

Back to Lia.

She'd made this trip herself such a short time ago. What had she been thinking as she'd taken off and circled over the islands? Had she been able to pick out his own island? It did look like an angel with her wings folded. The name would be perfect but would he be able to use it now or would it always remind him that he'd wrecked the best thing that had ever happened to him?

The lump in his throat made it hard to swallow.

Has she seen that yacht moored off Wildfire Island that looked a bit like his own? Had she thought about what she was leaving behind?

Had she thought about *him*?

She couldn't stop thinking about Sam.

Oh, for a while it had seemed easy enough. It had been a scene of typical Roselli family chaos with her surprise homecoming. Adriana had burst into tears, of course, and kept interrupting conversations to wrap

Lia in her arms or pinch her cheeks. Angel wouldn't let her out of her sight. Nico wasn't feeling great but it was Lia's reassurance that the side effects of the chemo were worth it that he'd been waiting to hear. As a bonus, her father was looking happier than she'd seen him in ages. He'd been for a job interview that day, he told her. He wouldn't hear anything before tomorrow but he was hopeful. Adriana was already preparing for a family celebration and phone calls were going back and forth as she issued invitations to Lia's siblings who weren't still living in the family house.

There'd been a bit of a blip in distraction when her mother had announced that Carla and Dino and their three children would be coming to join them for dinner tomorrow. She'd felt a pang of something like jealousy but a lot more poignant.

Carla had known she'd found 'the one'. So had Dino. And they'd gone on to find such happiness in their marriage.

But how often did a fairytale like that happen in real life?

Had she really believed it had happened to *her*?

Telling stories of her adventures made things even harder as the evening wore on.

'You were *underneath* a house blown over by the cyclone? All by yourself? *Mamma mia…*'

'I wasn't by myself. I was working with one of the doctors from the hospital. Sam.'

'Nice name.' The nudge from Fiona's elbow was meaningful. 'Was he good looking?'

'I guess…' Lia had to block the intimate detail with which Sam's face filled her mind. That unruly sun-bleached hair. Those gorgeous eyes. The texture of the skin on his jaw when he needed a shave and how different it was to that silky, soft spot on his neck. The shape of his lips when he smiled or…or when he was about to kiss her…

'Is he married?'

'Yep.' Well, that was the truth, wasn't it? He *was* married. Once.

And he'd been hurt and every cell in Lia's body had tried to send the message that she would never hurt him.

That she loved him far too much for that to ever be allowed to happen.

Her throat closed up at that point. She had to close her eyes to force the thoughts away.

'You're tired,' Adriana declared. 'And no wonder, with all that dangerous stuff you've been doing. Get to bed, *cara*.'

'You don't have to go to work tomorrow, do you?' Fiona asked.

'I don't think so. They're not expecting me back yet. I'll call Bruce in the morning and…'

And she'd have to think up a much better explanation for her early return than the one her family had been happy to accept.

'So you could come with me, then?'

Lia opened her eyes to find Fiona grinning at her. She had Angel on her lap and she cuddled her daughter. 'How good is that? Aunty Lia's going to come with us.'

'Come where?'

'Angel's hospital appointment. I need someone to come with me and help with the driving and wheelchair and everything. Dad needs to be here in case he's called in for another interview or something. Nico said he would but he's not feeling that great and you know what Mamma's like around hospitals. Guy's driving is...well...'

Lia held up her hand before an insult sparked off an argument. 'Of course I'll come. I'd love to.'

The more she had to do during the daytime, the better. The nights were going to be the worst because there'd be no distraction from where her thoughts were so determined to go. Back to Sam.

It hadn't been real, she reminded herself.

So why did it hurt *so* much?

It was the little girl in the wheelchair that Sam noticed first.

Yeah...right. As if the very shapely bottom stretching a close-fitting pair of jeans wouldn't have caught any red-blooded male eye, as the woman beside the wheelchair crouched to pick up a toy the child had dropped.

At least he raised his line of sight a little as she stood up, now caught by the fall of dark hair that reached the waistband of the jeans.

Something big clenched inside Sam's chest.

It looked just like Lia's hair when it was loose.

The woman was the same height as Lia, too. And her body was just as stunning.

Sam's steps faltered as the penny finally dropped.

'Lia?'

She turned so fast it made her hair swing. For a heartbeat he could swear he saw joy light up her features but then the shutters came down. There was no hint of a smile on her face.

'Sam. What on earth are you doing here?'

'I brought Felix over yesterday. He had some nerve damage that was getting worse and we couldn't do anything about it on Wildfire. I rang Graham Appleby and he said to bring him over immediately. It was too late for me to fly back by the time he'd been assessed and then Graham invited me to stay and watch the surgery this morning. I…' His words trailed away. He'd been talking too fast, hadn't he, and it was beginning to sound like he was making excuses for being in Lia's part of the world.

As if he would never have come voluntarily.

To see her or something.

Lia didn't even seem particularly interested. Her tone was very polite. 'How is Felix now?'

'He should make a full recovery. The surgery was amazing. I suspect you were right when you said that Professor Appleby was the best around.'

'Mmm…' Lia wasn't meeting his gaze. She was staring at something else.

'Is that *my* backpack?'

'Oh…yes. Jack asked me to bring it. He reckoned it would be easier for you to collect from here than anywhere else. I was just going to ask at Reception if it would be possible for them to look after it and…and here you are…'

'Yes. I came in with my sister to go to an occupational therapy appointment Angel had.' Lia stretched out her hand to take the pack. 'Thanks.'

She looked up as she took the bag and the connection hit Sam like a solid force. She knew he was thinking of that time on the beach together when he'd decided to name his island after her niece. Just before the sex that had been so mind-blowing that neither of them had minded the discomfort of the sand and bits of driftwood beneath them.

And she was hurting. Badly. He could feel that just as clearly and it cut through him like a knife.

He'd hurt her. The very least he could do was apologise but the crowded reception area of a large hospital was hardly the place.

Lia looked as if she would rather be a million miles away and another tall, dark-haired woman was rushing towards them, looking upset.

'Oh, God...Lia... You're not going to believe this. I can't start the car. I must have left the lights on and the battery's completely dead.'

'We'll ring Dad. He can come and jump-start us.'

'That'll take hours. Angel's tired enough as it is.'

'I could give you a lift home,' Sam offered. 'I've got a rental and I've missed the only flight that would have got me home today because the surgery took longer than expected. I'll have to reschedule one for the morning.'

The woman was staring at him. And then she turned her head to stare at Lia.

Lia sighed. 'This is Sam Taylor, one of the doctors from Wildfire Island. Sam, this is my sister Fiona. Angel's mum.'

Sam shook Fiona's hand. Then he stepped around the wheelchair so he could see the little girl's face.

'Hello, chicken. You must be Angel.'

She'd dropped her toy again so Sam crouched to pick it up. From the corner of his eye he could see the nonverbal communication going on between the sisters. Clearly, he had made an impression on Fiona Roselli but Lia wasn't playing. She looked uninterested. No. Worse than that. She was looking…angry.

The toy was an oversized stuffed clownfish and Sam made it swim towards Angel's arms.

'Bloop, bloop, bloop…'

Angel's mouth stretched into a grin wide enough to rival Lia's and her laughter was loud.

'Again,' she said, her words clearly difficult to enunciate. 'Do it again…'

This time he made it swim close enough for her to catch. Then he straightened and looked directly at Lia.

'Let me take you home,' he said quietly. 'Please?'

She held his gaze for only a moment before looking away. Had she seen how important this suddenly was for him? A chance to apologise? To try and put things right?

'That would be *awesome*,' Fiona said. 'Dad can bring one of the boys back to get the car later. Tomorrow, even.' She elbowed her sister. 'Say yes, Lia. I really, really don't want to be stuck here for hours, trying to keep Angel happy. You know how cranky she can get when she's bored. You have to say yes.'

'We wouldn't get the wheelchair into a rental car.'

'It's an SUV,' Sam said quietly. 'It wouldn't be a problem.'

Again, her gaze grazed his. Angel looked up at the adults around her and then threw her fish toy as far as she could.

'Again,' she demanded.

But it was Lia who stooped to pick up the toy. Her face was as tight as her voice as she looked up again.

'Fine,' she said. 'You can take us home. But only if

you're sure it's no bother.' She was turning away already. 'I'll go and get Angel's car seat.'

Fiona's eyes widened at her sister's tone. And then she looked at Sam and frowned. She had caught the undercurrent that something was going on here. Obviously, Lia hadn't told her family the real reason she'd left her FIFO post early but how long would it take for them to figure it out? Women, in particular, were so good at picking up on that kind of thing.

Sam swallowed. Was he about to step from the frying pan into the fire? What if the truth came out and he found himself facing the wrath of the entire Roselli family?

It was too late to back out now. And he didn't want to. This was a consequence and one he was more than prepared to face up to, if it meant he had a chance to talk to Lia.

'It's no bother,' he said. 'I'll bring the car round to the door.'

CHAPTER ELEVEN

IT WAS THE best thing that could have happened, being this close to Sam again.

It was also the worst thing that could have happened.

Lia's heart and her head were locked in a furious argument.

How could you possibly have agreed to this? the voice in her head was shouting. *You're stuck in a car with him, sitting close enough to touch. You have to listen to the sound of his voice. See his hands on the steering wheel, and you'll be thinking of what it feels like to be touched by those hands every time you catch sight of them. You can smell him, for heaven's sake. That wonderful, slightly musky scent that isn't any aftershave—it's the smell of the man you're stupidly still in love with...*

How could you possibly not *have agreed to this?*

It wasn't exactly a voice in her heart. More a feeling. An overwhelming one that was hard to put into words.

You saw that look in his eyes. He knows he's hurt you. He wants to fix things...

Angel, bless her, had decreed that Lia was to sit in the back seat beside her. Fiona was happy enough to take the front passenger seat after helping Sam stow the wheelchair, and then she was kept busy giving him directions to get through the city traffic. For a while Lia's head was appeased somewhat. This wouldn't take too long, it decided. He would drop them off and they'd say goodbye and that would be that. It would all be over. He'd probably apologise and maybe they'd agree that they would stay in touch. Stay friends…

But then Angel fell asleep and the traffic thinned enough for Fiona to become interested in other things.

'It must be like being on holiday permanently—living on a tropical island.'

'Not really,' Sam told her. 'The setting and the climate become normal after a while. I work, just the same as I would if I lived in a place like this. We've got a huge catchment area to look after and it's really spread out. We have clinics and emergencies on lots of islands and the hospital is almost always busy. Hectic, sometimes.'

Like it had been as the danger from that cyclone had died down, Lia remembered. She'd seen him, again and again, moving through the crowd of people who'd needed his medical expertise or sometimes just his reassurance. She'd been so aware of how much a part of this place he was. How much he was respected. And loved. And it had been at the end of that hectic, exhausting day that she'd known she was falling in love with Sam. That it had already happened, in fact, and nothing was ever going to change the way she felt about this man.

'We're often short of staff,' Sam continued. 'And we have to do a lot of extra stuff, like run laboratory tests ourselves. Plus, I'm involved in research. Right now we're rolling out clinical trials for a new encephalitis vaccine, which is really exciting…'

He sounded so passionate about his job. So sincere.

But her feelings *had* changed, Lia reminded herself. The shock of being accused of only being interested in his money. Of—almost—being accused of stealing it…

He didn't really accuse you of stealing his money, her heart whispered. *And after the disaster of his marriage, why wouldn't he have been suspicious of a woman who'd made no secret that money was important in her life?*

'Do you have physiotherapists at your hospital?' Fiona sounded excited.

'Only a visiting one. Lots of our specialist staff just come in once a fortnight or so to run clinics.' Sam turned his head to glance at Fiona. 'Why do you ask?'

'I've almost finished my training. I'm going to graduate as a physiotherapist soon, thanks to Lia.'

'Hardly.' It was the first time Lia had spoken since this car ride had begun. She had to clear her throat because it felt clogged—with tears that were trying to form? 'You did all the hard work yourself.'

'But I couldn't have even thought about going back to school unless you'd moved home to help look after Angel. You pretty much gave up your own life, apart from your job.'

The sound Lia made was supposed to be laughter. 'I have no life apart from my job. I love my job.'

'Me, too,' Fiona agreed. 'And wouldn't it be awesome

to be able to go and do it in a tropical paradise? Maybe I could be a visiting physio for Wildfire hospital.'

'Maybe you could.' But Sam's voice was wary.

'I'd love living on an island. Does your wife love it?'

'Sorry?'

'Lia said you were married.'

Lia cringed. She held her breath in the long silence that followed. She stared at Angel, trying to will her to wake up and distract everybody, but the little girl was sound asleep.

'I *was* married,' Sam said finally. 'A long time ago. It...didn't work out.'

'Ohh...' It was a meaningful sound and Fiona made it worse by craning her neck to turn and glare at Lia.

Lia turned and stared out of her window. She turned back after it seemed like enough time had passed to move on, only to catch Sam's gaze in the rear-vision mirror.

The silent communication was eloquent.

Did I really deserve that? To be reminded of the worst time of my life?

Yes. There was still a flash of that anger that came from feeling so betrayed. Maybe he hadn't really accused her of theft but he'd made it sound like he was comparing her to his ex-wife. That the possibility existed that she, too, couldn't be trusted.

No. He'd shared something private with her and she hadn't respected that. But she'd been protecting herself. It was far too raw to be ready to share what had gone on between herself and Sam so she'd had to put her sister off the scent.

Now she'd made things worse and the silence in the

car was very awkward. Fiona clearly knew that there was something not being said. Something huge. To her credit, she did try and change the subject.

'Isn't it great that Dad got called back for another interview? Being short-listed must be a good sign. I *so* hope he gets this job.'

'Your dad's out of work?' Sam sounded concerned.

'Has been for months.'

'That must be tough.'

'You're not wrong there,' Fiona confided. 'Our family would have sunk financially if it wasn't for Lia.'

Lia was cringing again. How much worse could this get? They were going to talk about *money*? She could hear his voice.

Money's so important to you, isn't it, Lia?

You didn't make any secret of it being why you came here in the first place, did you, Lia? For the money?

This was her fault as much as Sam's, wasn't it? She'd set herself up for the mistrust and then she'd run away without even trying to sort it out.

Was it possible that Sam was hurting as much as she was?

But he hadn't come to see her. He'd come with a patient. He'd been going to leave her backpack at the reception desk.

Fiona's voice was only a background buzz.

'Government help only goes so far, you know, especially when you've got a disabled kid in the family.'

'I can imagine.'

'That's why Lia took the job on your island. Mamma nearly had a heart attack when she heard about it but Lia really wanted the extra money, and you know why?'

'No,' Sam said very quietly. 'I don't.'

'Well, there's these new-generation callipers that are beyond anything the government will cover because they cost a bomb, but they look like exactly what Angel needs to be able to learn to walk. Oh…turn at the next left. We're almost home.'

He should have known.

Okay, so money was important to Lia but it wasn't for anything remotely selfish.

This gorgeous, incredibly smart, astonishingly courageous and passionate woman was devoting her life—and probably a large proportion of what she earned—to the people she loved.

Her family.

And *what* a family it was…

Sam was mobbed as soon as he'd parked his rented SUV in front of the sprawling old house with its wide veranda and open doors.

There were any number of people to help get Angel and all her accessories inside. To thank him for rescuing Fiona and Lia from their transport issues. The noise was overwhelming, in fact, and there were far too many names to try and remember. There were arguments going on, and not just between the young children who were running around.

'I'll take the chair.'

'Give it a rest, Nico. You're sick, remember?'

'Oh, let Guy do it. It's about time he did *something* useful around here.'

'*Fiona*. I heard that. Don't talk about your brother like that.'

'Fish. *Fish...*' Angel seemed to be well rested from her sleep in the car and was beaming at everyone.

'Dinner's ready. What's taking everybody so long?' Wiping her hands on her apron, the matriarch of this enormous family had finally pushed her way to the front of the group. 'Who are you?'

'Sam Taylor, Mrs Roselli.'

'He's a doctor, Mamma.' Fiona pulled another bag from the back of the car. Lia's backpack. 'He's the one Lia's being working with on the island.'

'What's he doing here, then?'

'He's Lia's friend, Mamma. And he was kind enough to give us a lift home.'

'It was a coincidence,' Sam put in. 'I happened to be at the hospital because I'd come over with a patient. It was...just lucky...'

He turned his head to where Lia was settling Angel back into her wheelchair. She probably didn't think it was lucky. But now she was surrounded by her family. Protected. The chances of being able to talk to her had just got a lot more remote.

'I'd better get going,' Sam said.

'*What?* Nonsense. You're staying for dinner. Come...' Lia's mother had a grip on his arm now. 'It's getting cold. Everybody come... Is this a celebration or what?'

Lia had straightened abruptly. 'We're celebrating? Dad? Did you get the job?'

'I start tomorrow.'

'Oh...' Lia flew into her father's arms. 'I'm so happy for you.'

The mob of people were moving and Sam had no choice but to go with them.

Down an overgrown path at the side of the house. Round a corner into a courtyard beneath a pergola that was smothered by a rampant grapevine that obscured many of the fairy-lights entwined with it. In the centre of the courtyard was a massive rustic-looking table that was laden with platters of food, bottles of wine and baskets of bread. At least a dozen large candles cast a warm glow over a scene that smelled as good as it looked.

'Sit,' Lia's father ordered. 'Here, at the head of the table. You are our guest. Lia…come and sit beside your friend.'

Sam was still having trouble putting names to faces. Fiona sat on the end of one of the long benches by the table, with Angel's wheelchair pulled up beside her. The small children squeezed in beside their parents. Carla and…Dino? Nico was easy to recognise because he was quieter than everyone else here and a bit too pale, but he'd forgotten who the young man was who had ear buds dangling around his neck, and there was another girl who had the same dark hair and eyes as Lia and Fiona. She was texting on her phone and it made Sam smile because he remembered Lia doing that when it wasn't appropriate, too. A poignant smile because he'd been wrong in the assumptions he'd made. But he'd apologised on the beach later that day, and look what that had led to…

Without thinking, he turned his head to where Lia was sitting quietly beside him.

'I'm sorry,' he said softly.

'What for?' The noise around the table as everyone helped themselves to food and admonished small children meant that nobody could hear these quiet words. Lia's sidelong glance was still full of hurt. Desperate, almost. 'Meeting me or losing your money?'

'It wasn't lost. The envelope was found under the hedge. Where we'd been resuscitating Keoni on your first day, remember?'

Lia was reaching out to accept a huge dish from one of her brothers.

'You have to try this,' she said loudly. 'Mamma's lasagne is the best there is.' She ladled some of the mix of pasta, meat and cheese onto his plate. 'And, of course I remember,' she added, but her voice was disconcertingly cool. 'I'm glad it turned up.'

Sam took a salad bowl coming from the other side of the table. 'And I could never be sorry about meeting you,' he said. 'Not in a million years.' He passed the salad bowl to Lia but still kept his hands on it as she took hold of it. The tips of her fingers were touching his. 'I'm sorry I said something so stupid. That let you believe something that isn't true.'

Her eyes were huge. 'What isn't true?'

Was anybody noticing what was going on at the end of this table? The noise level suggested not but Sam couldn't let this chance slip past in any case. It might be the only one he got.

'That none of it was real,' he said softly. 'It felt real to me. It still does.'

It *was* real.

Lia could see the love in Sam's eyes. She could feel how huge it was. How solid.

She wanted to throw her arms around his neck. To forgive and forget everything about the horrible hours since she'd walked out of the staffroom at Wildfire hospital. To start again, with this new understanding of each other that would bring them so much closer and give them a foundation that had no secrets.

But that needed complete honesty.

And trust.

'But you were right,' she said, in little more than a whisper. 'Money *is* important to me.'

They were both ignoring their food. Sam's gaze still had hold of Lia's and there was a gentle curve to the corners of his mouth.

'Only because of what you need it for. Your family. I get that, Lia. I know how blessed you are.'

'Eat…' The command came from Adriana Roselli, who was reaching for a basket of bread. 'What's wrong with my food? Here…you need bread.'

'Nothing's wrong, Mamma. It's delicious.' Lia scooped up a forkful of the lasagne. 'It's my favourite.'

'Mine, too,' Sam said. 'Now…'

He was grinning and everybody laughed. And then they started firing questions at Sam.

'How come it was Lia who went under the squashed house?' Guy asked. 'Wasn't that dangerous?'

'I didn't want her to,' Sam said. 'It *was* dangerous. But she was the one who was small enough to get through the gap and…and she wasn't going to let me stop her.'

'That's our Lia.' Nico nodded.

'Sam came as far as he could,' Lia put in. 'There was a tiny baby we needed to get out and Sam put her inside his shirt to keep her safe.'

The memory made her eyes fill and any remnants of anger she'd been trying to hold on to evaporated.

She loved this man. With all her heart and soul.

Her appetite had gone. Instead, she sat quietly, watching her family as they got to know Sam a little better. They were impressed. Ready to welcome him as more than a guest?

I know how blessed you are...

There had been a note of longing in Sam's voice. It took her back to that moment she'd been with him when she'd been holding Hika's baby and Sefina's little boy in her arms. When she'd felt the loneliness of what was missing in Sam's life and had wanted to hold him close to her heart and never let him go. When she'd known that, as far as her heart was concerned, he already was a part of her own family.

Angel's head was drooping, down at the far end of this long table, and Lia's father pushed his plate away and stood up.

'Let me take her. I'll put her to bed.'

It took time to undo the safety harness that kept Angel in her wheelchair and Lia could sense that Sam was about to get up to help lift her.

'They can manage,' she said quietly.

'But I want to help.'

'I know. But there's nothing you need to do. We're used to it.'

'There is something I could do.' Sam caught Lia's hand. 'Let me get those new callipers for her. The ones that might help her walk.'

Lia stiffened. 'We don't need your money, Sam.' She pulled her hand free of his. Pushed herself to her feet.

Were they back to square one?

Sam stood up, as well.

And everybody else froze. For probably the first time in history the entire Roselli family was completely silent, staring at Sam and Lia, who were staring at each other.

'Our family takes care of itself,' Lia said. 'We don't need charity.'

'I know that. But…I'm part of this, Lia. You know I am…'

'*Mamma mia…*' The whisper was loud enough for all to hear. 'What's going on here?'

Sam turned to face the whole family. Lia's father was standing behind her mother, with Angel in his arms. Fiona was standing beside him, her hand covering her open mouth. Her voice was muffled.

'I *knew* it…Lia, you have some explaining to do.'

'No.' Sam cleared his throat. 'It's me who has some explaining to do. Mr and Mrs Roselli, I haven't known your daughter for very long but I've learned a lot of things about her. I've learned that she loves her family so much she'll do whatever it takes to support you all. I've learned that she's the bravest and smartest person I've ever met and, most importantly, I've learned that…' he turned from the table to look directly at Lia '… I love her. That I always will. That she's the person I want to spend the rest of my life with. The woman I intend to marry if I'm lucky enough that she wants that, too.'

Lia was drowning in his eyes. Bursting with a joy that was going to escape as tears at any moment. Her mother was already crying—she could hear it.

'I love you, too, Sam. You're already a part of my family. I can't imagine the rest of my life without you in it.'

'Awesome,' Guy said. 'Can we come and see that squashed house? And the mine that exploded?'

'Shut up, Guy,' someone hissed.

'I knew it,' Fiona said again. She was crying, too. 'Oh, I'm so happy for you, Lia. It's about time...'

Angel had woken up in her grandfather's arms. She beamed at Sam.

'Fish...' she demanded.

'*No...*' Adriana was mopping her face with the corner of her apron. 'No, no, no...this is all too soon. Too fast.'

Carla and Dino were grinning.

'Where have we heard that before?' Carla said.

Lia took Sam's hand in hers and turned to face her family. She smiled at Carla but her lips wobbled. Then her gaze took in her whole family.

'We have heard it before and you all know it can be true. It's true this time, too.'

'What is?' Sam sounded bewildered.

Lia turned back to him. She let go of his hand so that she could wrap her arms around his neck. Could stand on tiptoe and kiss him in front of everybody.

'When you know, you just know,' she said softly.

'Oh...' Sam's lips touched hers so gently she could feel them moving as he spoke. 'Yes. That *is* true...*I* know...'

'So do I.'

And then there was no way either of them could say anything else as their kiss took them into a space that only they could share. They could hear the joyous sound of a family celebrating around them as they welcomed their newest member.

They could feel the love.

But this…this was all their own and it was real.

Real enough to last forever.

* * * * *

MILLS & BOON®

Hardback – April 2016

ROMANCE

The Sicilian's Stolen Son	Lynne Graham
Seduced into Her Boss's Service	Cathy Williams
The Billionaire's Defiant Acquisition	Sharon Kendrick
One Night to Wedding Vows	Kim Lawrence
Engaged to Her Ravensdale Enemy	Melanie Milburne
A Diamond Deal with the Greek	Maya Blake
Inherited by Ferranti	Kate Hewitt
The Secret to Marrying Marchesi	Amanda Cinelli
The Billionaire's Baby Swap	Rebecca Winters
The Wedding Planner's Big Day	Cara Colter
Holiday with the Best Man	Kate Hardy
Tempted by Her Tycoon Boss	Jennie Adams
Seduced by the Heart Surgeon	Carol Marinelli
Falling for the Single Dad	Emily Forbes
The Fling That Changed Everything	Alison Roberts
A Child to Open Their Hearts	Marion Lennox
The Greek Doctor's Secret Son	Jennifer Taylor
Caught in a Storm of Passion	Lucy Ryder
Take Me, Cowboy	Maisey Yates
His Baby Agenda	Katherine Garbera

0316 GEN STD HB

MILLS & BOON®

Large Print – April 2016

ROMANCE

The Price of His Redemption	Carol Marinelli
Back in the Brazilian's Bed	Susan Stephens
The Innocent's Sinful Craving	Sara Craven
Brunetti's Secret Son	Maya Blake
Talos Claims His Virgin	Michelle Smart
Destined for the Desert King	Kate Walker
Ravensdale's Defiant Captive	Melanie Milburne
The Best Man & The Wedding Planner	Teresa Carpenter
Proposal at the Winter Ball	Jessica Gilmore
Bodyguard...to Bridegroom?	Nikki Logan
Christmas Kisses with Her Boss	Nina Milne

HISTORICAL

His Christmas Countess	Louise Allen
The Captain's Christmas Bride	Annie Burrows
Lord Lansbury's Christmas Wedding	Helen Dickson
Warrior of Fire	Michelle Willingham
Lady Rowena's Ruin	Carol Townend

MEDICAL

The Baby of Their Dreams	Carol Marinelli
Falling for Her Reluctant Sheikh	Amalie Berlin
Hot-Shot Doc, Secret Dad	Lynne Marshall
Father for Her Newborn Baby	Lynne Marshall
His Little Christmas Miracle	Emily Forbes
Safe in the Surgeon's Arms	Molly Evans

MILLS & BOON®

Hardback – May 2016

ROMANCE

Morelli's Mistress	Anne Mather
A Tycoon to Be Reckoned With	Julia James
Billionaire Without a Past	Carol Marinelli
The Shock Cassano Baby	Andie Brock
The Most Scandalous Ravensdale	Melanie Milburne
The Sheikh's Last Mistress	Rachael Thomas
Claiming the Royal Innocent	Jennifer Hayward
Kept at the Argentine's Command	Lucy Ellis
The Billionaire Who Saw Her Beauty	Rebecca Winters
In the Boss's Castle	Jessica Gilmore
One Week with the French Tycoon	Christy McKellen
Rafael's Contract Bride	Nina Milne
Tempted by Hollywood's Top Doc	Louisa George
Perfect Rivals...	Amy Ruttan
English Rose in the Outback	Lucy Clark
A Family for Chloe	Lucy Clark
The Doctor's Baby Secret	Scarlet Wilson
Married for the Boss's Baby	Susan Carlisle
Twins for the Texan	Charlene Sands
Secret Baby Scandal	Joanne Rock

0416 GEN STD HB